STEVE HEUZINKVELD

PREDATORS OF THE FALL

THE FALL SERIES BOOK FOUR

Dedicated to Christopher Paul Diggle,
whose work ethic and passion for progress
is a constant inspiration.

Foreword

While this story is based on real locations throughout the United States, I have used fictitious names for some towns and neighborhoods, so that I can change certain aspects of these locations for the sake of the story.

Thank you, and enjoy!

CHAPTER 1

"Stay down, you son of a bitch," Riley Armstrong snarled in the ear-ringing silence of the desolate neighborhood.

She kept her pistol trained on the stilled body in the middle of the street, even though her gun's slide had already cocked back, airing out the empty chamber.

"Nice shot," Heather Seabrook panted huskily from the suburban street's sidewalk, eyeing the trickle of blood staining the asphalt, her combat knife in hand.

"Go slow," Riley urged, holstering her spent pistol before reaching for her own blade.

"Nah, I think we're good," Heather replied, straightening up. Her travel-worn boots tramped through stalks of overgrown grass as she stepped out onto the road. "Looks like we're finally having fresh meat tonight."

Long ears twitching at her approach, the injured hare bolted, even with a dose of hot lead in its side.

"FUCK!!" Heather threw her knife at the critter, the blade missing its mark and clattering harmlessly in the hare's wake. "He's going for the cars!"

Seeking shelter, the wounded animal darted underneath a

long-forgotten pile-up of vehicles blocking the intersection ahead.

"That was our last bullet," Riley icily reminded her as they split up to search the wreckage.

"We'll get you more when we get to Josh's house," Heather replied with a bitter sigh. "By now, Taylor and the others have probably scavenged enough supplies to get you all the way home."

Riley bit her doubtful tongue, turning her focus back towards their prey.

Dropping to her gloved hands and knees on one side of the pile-up, she scanned underneath the tangled mass of jagged metal, warped wheels and broken glass.

Her breath froze in her chest as she came face to face with a long-dead corpse's skull, its hollow eyes staring back into Riley's, with its decomposing lips frozen in a macabre grin.

The skeleton's ragged remains were just as twisted as the intertwined chunks of chassis above, the cadaver crushed and contorted either from the initial crash, or from the scavengers that had picked the body clean afterwards.

The farther west that the two women traveled, the more frequently they encountered chaotic scenes from the early days of the apocalypse – back when people still had enough fuel to hurl themselves through a windshield.

But looking at the asphalt in between the bodies, there was still no sign of the hare.

"Any luck?" Riley rose to her feet and wiped the dust off her brown plaid shirt and jeans, as if her clothes had been clean to begin with.

"Nothing but old bones," Heather called back from the other side. "If he bleeds out under there, we're not getting him back."

"Shit," Riley rubbed the back of her neck as she sized up their surroundings, searching for another strategy.

Beyond the jumble of crumpled sedans, station wagons and pickup trucks, there was a charred husk of a burnt-out firetruck lying on its side, the debris from the wreck diagonally blocking off the intersection from street corner to street corner.

Only one other road was clear from the obstruction.

Riley's head cocked slightly as her hazel eyes settled on the row of townhouses along the next street, and the lane of garages behind them.

If they could flush out the hare, then there were only two ways for it to run.

"Alright, here's what we'll do," Riley spoke over her shoulder as she put away her knife. She set one of her hiking boots on the rear end of a mangled pickup truck, before turning to Heather, "You stay over here. If he comes out on my side, you take the alley and try to cut him off at the next intersection. Ready?"

"Hold on," Heather tightened the straps of her backpack as she geared up for another run. "Okay. Let's get this furry fucker."

Riley climbed up onto the back of the pickup truck, her boots swishing through a shallow pool of stagnant water and slimy algae. Holding on to the pickup's cabin so that she wouldn't lose her balance, she began stomping with one foot on the rusty cargo bed.

The *bangs* and *clangs* reverberated around the derelict neighborhood, with the whole vehicular jigsaw puzzle groaning and shuddering underneath her.

Rocking haphazardly in the back of the truck, Riley kept her eyes trained on the intersection.

Watching.

3

Waiting.

The hare bolted.

"GO!!" she shouted, leaping off the truck.

Hitting the ground running, Riley turned the corner, hounding after their next meal.

A streak of red hair flashed in the corner of her eye as Heather dashed into the alley.

The street was empty, other than a few feral cats watching from the row of townhouses, their yellow eyes following the chase with keen interest.

Riley was gaining on the hare, the animal slowed by its pronounced limp.

Veering to the far side of the road as they neared the next intersection, she steered the hare from behind, intent on running their prey straight into Heather.

Heart pounding in her ears, Riley's shadow loomed over the hare as they turned the corner.

But Heather was missing.

Too slow, Riley snorted in between breaths, before ducking her head down into her chest, keeping her gaze firmly locked on the hare's tail bobbing up and down. *Fuck it. I'll get him myself.*

Another streak of red hair flashed in the corner of her eye as she zipped past the alley.

But this time, it was different.

Heather was slumped over on the ground.

And she wasn't moving.

CHAPTER 2

"Heather, what the fuck!?" Riley Armstrong called from the alley's entrance, her eyes still following the hare as it half-ran, half-limped up the street. "He's getting away!"

No response.

Riley squinted her eyes into the garage lane as she caught her breath.

"Heather!" she whispered another shout into the alley.

Still no response.

Half of the alley's roller doors stood open.

Light from the afternoon sun flooded the alley intermittently, the rear doors of each garage softly creaking open and shut.

Riley's shoulders shivered involuntarily as a sudden chill ran up her spine.

It was the perfect place for an ambush.

Especially for two women who had just fired their last bullet.

Forgetting their feebly fleeing prey, her sharp eyes traced over the dusty sedans and dead pot plants lining the alley. The alley was strewn with milk crates and cardboard boxes and other windborne trash curling with the breeze.

There were too many places for an attacker to hide.

Pretending that her gun still had ammo wasn't an option either, not if someone had been listening in on their conversation.

Glancing over her shoulder, Riley drew her combat knife from the strap on her thigh.

Standing at the mouth of the alley, her eyes slid sideways, going from the row of roller doors to the tall wooden fence on the other side.

Clenching the hilt of her blade in between her teeth, Riley took two quick steps towards the wooden wall, dug the spiky grooves of her hiking boots into the corner fence-post, and hoisted herself up.

Perched on top of the fence, she examined the alley from her new vantage point, but Heather seemed to be the only other person around.

The lawn of the abandoned house on the other side of the fence was overgrown, with tall stalks of grass reaching up to reclaim a rusty swing set, a weather-beaten shed, and a cobweb-covered clothesline.

But the backyard was otherwise empty.

Either the ambushers had picked good hiding places, or Riley just wasn't looking hard enough.

She summoned her resolve, adjusting the straps of her backpack, before easing the toes of her boots down onto the fence's middle railing.

Shuffling sideways along the fence, hand over hand, Riley kept her head on a swivel, peering into each one of the open garages across the alley, while also checking over her shoulder to watch the house behind her.

"Ugh, my head," Heather groaned groggily, brushing back her red hair as she pushed herself upright in the alley. She drew in a sharp breath, "Oh, fuck – Riley!!"

"Up here," she whispered down from above, the handle of her combat knife still clenched in between her teeth as she kept a wary lookout on their surroundings.

"Who the fuck leaves shit like this lying around?" Heather hissed in a combination of pain and anger, rising up to struggle with a long wooden plank caught just below her knee.

"How deep is it?" Riley leaned over the fence to examine the spiked board spanning the width of the alley.

A few feet behind Heather, a loose length of fishing cord was spread across the ground, tied between a dead pot plant and a fence-post. The wooden plank that the tripwire had triggered was studded with the metal teeth of garden stakes.

And one of them had embedded itself into the lean meat of Heather's lower leg.

"Deep enough to hurt like a bitch," the fiery redhead grimaced. Her husky voice turned hollow, howling in agony as she wrenched herself free, "FUUUUUCK!!"

Strips of flesh and fabric hung from the bloody garden stake as Heather hobbled towards the fence, the echoes of her anguish fading into the void of the abandoned neighborhood.

Shrugging off her backpack, she slumped onto the ground, rummaging through her supplies for something to staunch the wound.

Still keeping watch from above, Riley's gaze went from the spiked board, to the tripwire, to the pile-up in the street.

Somebody had used this location to their advantage.

Why climb over the car crash when there's a perfectly good alley to walk through?

For one fleeting moment, Riley flashed back to when she and Hayden Marsh had laid a trap for Braxton Shepherd's people back in Nebraska.

"Whoever set this up," Riley glanced one last time over her shoulder, before climbing down into the alley beside Heather, "We should get moving before they come back."

CHAPTER 3

Hefting a black leather office chair over her shoulder, Riley cautiously picked her path through one townhouse's overgrown grass back towards the alley.

"You couldn't find a wheelbarrow for me?" Heather bristled at the sight of the office chair. She had dressed her wound with a sanitary pad, packing it with a spare shirt and using a pair of butchered socks to hold it all in place. "Fuck me – even a shopping cart would've been better."

As it turned out, Riley had spotted a wheelbarrow in one of the backyards, but there was no way that she was going to lug Heather all the way over to her cousin's house – wherever that was.

"Fine, I'll just put this back where I found it," Riley stood underneath the roller door of the garage closest to Heather. "Maybe you can crawl the rest of the way back to Taylor and Josh instead."

"Bitch," the fiery redhead let out a pained chuckle as she rose up on her good leg. "You don't even know how far I'd have to drag myself."

"It'd be fun to watch though," she dropped the chair beside

Heather, holding it steady for her.

"Yeah, for a sadist," Heather scowled back, hugging her wounded leg to her chest as she began scooting herself backwards out of the alley. "At least tell me you got the hare?"

Riley shook her head ruefully, having come within inches of diving distance.

"Just my fucking luck," Heather muttered bitterly, checking her rear as she backed herself out into the street. "I'm gonna be rolling up to my cousin's house with one bad leg and nothing to show for it."

"That's what you get for wanting to do something nice," Riley gave her a dry smirk as she walked slowly beside Heather, both of them still scanning the empty neighborhood for any signs of movement.

Having been separated from Taylor for the past three months, Heather had wanted to surprise what was left of her family by bringing in a fresh kill for dinner.

Now, it seemed that the two women weren't the only predators stalking the neighborhood.

And whoever had set up the spike trap in the alley – rigged to strike a victim just below knee height – it was clear that they weren't hunting for small game.

CHAPTER 4

"Don't tell me you're lost," Riley shot a sidelong glance at Heather. "We passed this street a while back."

As common as the scenes of anarchy from the early days of the apocalypse were becoming, the sight was still impossible to forget.

A semicircular score of bodies were scattered around an intersection bordering a small strip mall. Bullet holes and scorch marks scarred brick, concrete and asphalt alike.

Stacks of sandbags lined the roof from the gun store on one end, and traveled all the way to the hardware store on the other side, while blockades of debris and barbed wire had been strewn haphazardly across the parking lot.

Apparently, the local store owners had formed an alliance against any raiders trying to storm the strip mall for supplies. With the convenience store in the middle, the alliance probably would have lasted for quite a while, at least up until one of the attackers had decided to ram a delivery truck through the gun store's brick wall.

"Just making sure we aren't being followed," Heather stared over her shoulder as she navigated her office chair's wheels in between the bodies.

"Well, you'd be the one to know," Riley breathed shallow as she scanned the decomposing faces for a second time, making sure that each body was well and truly dead. "You've been facing backwards this whole time. If you haven't seen anything by now, I think we're g– hey, watch that arm."

"Thanks," Heather sighed half-heartedly, scooting sideways before continuing her one-legged reverse up the avenue. "Well, I can pretty much fucking guarantee that we're not going with you all the way to Cali now, even if you *could* manage to convince me."

"Who said I wanted you to come?" Riley gave her a small snort as they left the grisly landmark.

"Don't give me that shit," Heather glanced up at her with a chuckle. "You've been hoping I'd come with you ever since we left Colorado. You know you'd have a *significantly* better chance at getting there alive with my group than if you went out on your own."

"I would," Riley admitted with a swallow, avoiding the gaze of her striking green eyes.

"It's probably not gonna count for much now," Heather began as they hit the next block, "But I was waiting to see how my group was going with the scavenging runs out here. If Taylor was coming back empty-handed every time, I'd just tell them to grab their shit and head out west with you – at least for a while. They're only stuck in this town because they're waiting on me. But if business is good around here, I'd be waving at you from the front window saying *good luck, bitch*."

"And now?" Riley shot a skeptical glance at Heather's injured leg.

"*Good luck, bitch*," she echoed with a shrug. "Even if the whole state's already been picked clean, I'm not going anywhere until this shit heals up first."

"At least you know there's still some animals around here you can hunt," Riley supposed, slightly crestfallen. "Well, not you. But your friends can."

"Fuck off," Heather kicked herself sideways towards a housing estate. "Come on, this way."

Riley shook her head at the contradiction, but she followed her all the same.

She had her doubts as to whether Heather's group was actually waiting for her.

After all, Taylor was the youngest of their friends. And from what Riley had seen of her back in Kansas, she was also the most irrational. If times had gotten tough and her voice wasn't being heard, Taylor would have been faced with the decision between waiting for her sister, hungry and alone, or sticking to safety in numbers.

Riley could guess what she would have done – whatever her sister would have wanted.

And that was if they had even made it to Utah.

But she kept her doubts to herself.

Because as valid as they were, she still needed to stock up on her supplies before she could continue her journey back to Redhurst.

So when Heather skidded to a stop in the middle of the street, her eyes set on one particular house, Riley hoped that she was wrong.

CHAPTER 5

"Taylor?" Heather called from the side of the road, staring at the modest house that was as plain-Jane as any other. "Josh? It's me – Heather. Don't shoot."

"That's one hell of a password," Riley gave a small snort as she held up her gloved hands, hoping that nobody inside the house had an itchy trigger finger.

"Who the fuck uses passwords?" Heather glanced up at Riley as she scooted herself backwards towards the driveway. She paused for a moment, realizing that she'd be facing away from the house on their approach, and turning her back on anyone who would be able to recognize her. "Shit. You're gonna have to push me."

"I guess a couple yards couldn't hurt," Riley supposed, dropping one hand to the back of Heather's chair, her other hand still up in the air. She peered at the house again. "I thought they would've boarded up the windows by now."

"You mean just like our house back in Kansas?" Heather spoke over her shoulder as they turned past the mailbox. "That was another one of Taylor's stupid ideas. I'm guessing those boarded windows were how you found us in the first place."

"That, and the two bodies you guys left out in the street," Riley replied as they trundled up the garden path towards the concrete porch's steps.

"Looks like Josh talked them outta doing the same shit here, at least," Heather gazed at the house's empty windows. "Where the fuck is everybody though? Josh!? Taylor!!"

The house was as silent as the rest of the street.

Despite the heat of the afternoon spring sun, a rash of gooseflesh budded up Riley's arms.

She glanced back over her shoulder, feeling like they were being watched.

Stopping at the porch's bottom step, Riley lowered both arms, one hand magnetically drawn towards the combat knife strapped to her thigh.

"They're not gonna shoot at me if I knock on the door, right?" Riley asked as she stepped out from behind Heather.

"Last time Taylor saw you," Heather eased herself out of the black leather office chair, "You and your friends stole half our shit. You better give me a hand up these steps."

Draping one arm around Riley's shoulders for support, Heather hopped up onto the porch. Behind them, the office chair rolled and spun down the garden path, before toppling over into the overgrown grass by the curb.

With her green eyes lingering on Riley's, Heather gingerly set down her injured leg, planting both boots on the porch, wanting to radiate strength for the long-awaited reunion with her little sister.

Standing tall, she rapped her knuckles against the wooden door.

The two women waited side by side with bated breaths, listening for footsteps, a quiet mutter, or even the sound of

15

a gun cocking.

But there was nothing.

Just silence.

Riley's gloved fingers brushed the hilt of her combat knife.

She fondled the strap for a moment before trying the door handle.

It was unlocked.

The door's hinges creaked a forlorn welcome as they peered into the empty hallway.

"Taylor?" Heather called, craning her neck inside. "Josh?" Forgetting her leg wound, she stepped over the threshold, before grimacing in pain, "Son of a bitch! Fuck that piece of shit hare... Riley, are you done gawking yet?"

Cocking an eyebrow at the fiery redhead, Riley hauled her inside.

Limping around with three legs and one arm around each other, the pair of women checked the house.

Nobody in the front room.

Nobody in the dining area.

Nobody in the kitchen.

Riley was beginning to think that her unvoiced doubts had come to life.

Heather's group hadn't made it over to Utah after all.

There would be no stash of scavenged supplies for Riley to restock her backpack.

No food to bolster her meager provisions.

No bullets to reload her empty pistol.

"Come on, come on..." Heather breathed as they hobbled towards the back bedroom, her eyes poring over the pair of single beds inside.

The blankets had been thrown open, as if the occupants had

woken up and left in a hurry – but whether that had been nine hours ago or nine months ago, neither Riley nor Heather could guess.

"Riley, check the laundry closet," Heather took off towards the master bedroom, hopping down the hallway on her good leg. "If they're out on a supply run, that'll be where the food is."

"Not in the pantry?" Riley called in her wake, furrowing her eyebrows.

"Why the fuck would they leave food in the pantry?" Heather hissed in her frustration, before disappearing into the bedroom.

With a begrudging sigh, Riley searched the laundry closet. She opened the metal door underneath the sink. She even looked inside the washing machine.

But aside from a few bottles of cleaning chemicals, the laundry was empty.

The shelves in the kitchen pantry weren't any better.

Even a cockroach had died of starvation.

"Did you find anything?" Riley found Heather slumped on the couch in the front room, staring out the window.

"It doesn't make any sense," Heather shook her head, her gaze dropping to the floor. "I told Taylor to be here. She should fucking be here. Josh should fucking be here. Where the fuck are they?"

"Maybe your cousin left town back when this whole mess started," Riley ventured, trying to sound more reassuring than she felt. "Taylor and the rest of your group must have come through, scavenged everything that they could get their hands on, and then left when the supplies dried up. Did you see if she left you a note?"

"I'd be surprised if she could think that far ahead," Heather pinched the bridge of her nose in thought. "Okay, so Josh is gone. I can live with that. Taylor and the others would've been on foot from Kansas, but after your little detour, we ended up taking the long way to get here. They should've been here by now. Unless..."

"The soldiers picked them up back in Colorado?" Riley guessed the end of her sentence.

"Or, they're still on their way," Heather narrowed her eyes at Riley, before hugging her wounded leg to her chest and turning her gaze to the ceiling with a huff. "Whatever happened, they're not here, and I need a proper bandage. Why don't you look around for a first aid kit and some clean linen? I'll get started on dinner."

Riley stood motionless by the couch, watching as she rummaged through her backpack.

Even if the rest of Heather's group was still on their way, they'd only have the supplies that they were carrying on their backs – not enough to spare for Riley's journey west, regardless of how well she had gotten to know Heather over the past few months.

Both women had agreed that they would travel together as far as Josh's house, and now it seemed that their mutually beneficial arrangement was coming to an end.

Just without the light at the end of the tunnel that they had been hoping for.

Is it even worth staying? Riley wondered, her eyes tracing over Heather's injured leg. *She needs me now more than I need her. What was that she was gonna say? Good luck, bitch.*

"Riley?" Heather tested, her usual tone of nonchalance sounding a little needier than normal as both women realized her vulnerability.

"It's just – I was hoping..." she faltered, glancing at Heather's half-empty bag of cat biscuits with dread. Riley bit her bottom lip before going over to the window. "Man, that hare would've made this shit-show a hell of a lot easier to swallow."

"Look at me," Heather sat up on the couch, setting aside their meager dinner. She bore her eyes into the back of Riley's skull. "I know what you're thinking. Don't you fucking dare leave me like this."

Riley rubbed the back of her neck as she gazed up at the orange tint in the clouds.

It was getting late now.

And Heather needed an answer.

Riley was about to turn back around, when a flash of movement caught her eye.

"Hold on," she stared outside, her breath fogging the glass. "Did you see that?"

"Don't do this," Heather hung her head, blinking down at her leg. "Please, don't do this."

"I thought you said the rest of your group was around our age?" Riley's keen gaze zeroed in on a kid wearing a yellow shirt across the street.

He gaped back at her as he tried – poorly – to hide behind a tree.

"You don't have to make up a fucking story," Heather bristled, glowering up at her from the couch. "At least have the balls to – wait – what the fuck? Who's that?"

She hobbled over to the window beside Riley, the kid soon disappearing from view, realizing that his cover was blown.

"Looks like we're not the only ones here," Riley scanned the rest of the street for any other people.

"Maybe he lives somewhere in this neighborhood," Heather

supposed, before her chest swelled with hope again. "He might know what happened to Josh. Or maybe... maybe Taylor found a better place somewhere else in town, and she told him to keep tabs on this house until I came looking for her. It makes sense – I mean, why risk leaving a note for just anybody to find?"

"I doubt the shit outta that," Riley's thoughts jumped to the more likely scenario. "He's probably the spotter for whoever set up that trap."

CHAPTER 6

"Hey, kid, stop!" Riley Armstrong shouted in between wheezes for breath, doggedly trotting after him as he dashed around yet another intersection. "I just wanna talk!"

But by the time she had caught up and turned the corner, he was already gone.

Panting heavily while thumbing at the stitch in her side, Riley quickly scanned her surroundings.

The kid had run her ragged across town.

She had no idea where she was now, and the sun was already starting to set.

What the hell am I doing? Riley chided herself in the middle of the street.

If the kid had any connection to whoever had been laying traps in the area, for all she knew, she could have been running straight into another one.

Given that she hadn't impaled her leg on a spiked board yet, it was probably safe to say that he wasn't an immediate threat – but that still didn't explain why he had been following them in the first place.

Riley squinted at the trees and fences and forgotten cars lining the street.

Seeing no sign of the kid, she spun on her heel and went back the way she came.

She couldn't afford to risk chasing after him any longer.

He knew the area.

And she was losing the light.

The muscles in her thighs burned as she retraced her steps, but at least her fatigue wouldn't stop her if she needed to start running again. Now that she had called off the chase, it was her turn to constantly check back over her shoulder, making sure that nobody was following her.

Not that it would matter anyway – the kid already knew where the pair of women had holed up for the night.

She had to get back to Heather.

They needed to find a new place to sleep.

With her shadow growing long on the ground, Riley paused at the next intersection. Extending one arm towards the westering sun, she counted the number of fingers in between the sun and the horizon.

On the road from Colorado, she had learned that each finger was worth around fifteen minutes of daylight, but with her gloves on, it was more like twenty.

She had less than that.

Kicking her legs back into a stubborn jog, Riley kept her eyes peeled for any movement from the surrounding houses as she turned her thoughts inwards, distracting herself from the stinging stitch in her side.

There was no denying that Heather was a liability now.

But if the roles had been reversed, would she have left Riley to fend for herself?

Probably, Riley admitted with a weary grin. *Definitely, if it came down to a choice between me and Taylor.*

But that didn't cheapen the lessons of selflessness taught to her by the likes of Keith Bowman and Virge Norton, who had both been willing to put their lives on the line for Riley and her mother.

Even Katanya Grady had proven to be an unlikely ally in the months following the asteroid's impact, although Riley had always felt like Katanya had just been paying off the moral debt of leaving her stranded on the side of a freeway.

It was different with Heather though – Riley had broken into her house, stolen half of her supplies, and caused the Seabrook sisters to split up in their search for her.

Now Riley was the one carrying a moral debt.

And she couldn't leave Heather until it was settled.

Not if she wanted to lose what was left of her humanity.

Riley paused at the next intersection, frowning as she peered left and right.

Neither road seemed familiar.

"Fuck," she panted, glancing back over her shoulder.

She had taken a wrong turn.

CHAPTER 7

Riley was lost in the labyrinth of suburban streets, and dusk was already beginning to settle in as the sun shone its final rays from the horizon.

Trying to find her way back in the dark would be even worse, but she didn't have a choice – if the kid was a spotter for the locals, Heather wouldn't stand a chance by herself. With her wounded leg, she could barely stand at all.

Adjusting the straps of her backpack, Riley drew her combat knife.

Keeping the sunset on her left, she silently hoped that she would eventually come across a landmark that she could recognize.

Her hiking boots scuffed the asphalt as twilight descended on the suburban wasteland.

Lifeless streetlamps loomed overhead like dreadful specters of the past, lamenting the loss of their inner light. Forever forced to spend their nights in darkness, they loathed the lone traveler, glowering down at her through the gloom.

Dark houses played tricks on Riley's mind, somber silhouettes standing behind windows, staring in silence as they waited for her to let down her guard. But when she snapped her gaze towards them, the shadows shifted back into the shapes of drapes, armchairs, shelves and bunk beds.

As eerie as the deserted streets were, Riley maintained a steady walking pace.

If she ran through the twilight, she would risk missing a movement in the overgrown grass lining both sides of the road, or she wouldn't be able to distinguish a second set of footfalls from her own.

But if she went too slow, she would only be inviting the night's predators to draw closer, right up until they were within striking range.

An unbidden image flashed into her mind – the big yellow eyes of the monstrous mountain lion that had mauled Hayden Marsh – and Riley glanced back over her shoulder, tightly clenching the handle of her combat knife.

Her pupils dilated as she glimpsed a hulking obstruction lying across the road in the distance.

The firetruck, she realized, recognizing the same row of townhouses lining the empty street on the next block.

Finally back in familiar territory, she shrank to the sidewalk as she cautiously approached the next intersection.

Stealing from one defunct utility pole to the next, she crept around the corner, acutely aware of the fact that there might be somebody else skulking through the abandoned neighborhood, checking on their traps.

She crouched beside the dusty hood of a forgotten sedan, chancing a glance into the cluttered alley behind the row of townhouses.

The spiked wooden board had been left untouched, still spanning the width of the alley.

Seeing no sign of anybody else in the area, Riley stood up from behind cover, breathing out the tension in her muscles as she picked up the pace again.

She was making far better time on her own than she had with Heather, although that was only because she didn't have to wait for the woman's office chair to trundle up the street.

At the rate that she was going, Riley figured that she'd be back at Josh's house just after dusk. And once she got there, she and Heather could use the cover of darkness to find another place to stay.

And hopefully it would be a place that didn't have any creepy kids staring at them from across the street.

Riley's feet froze to the ground as something caught her eye.

A faint glow was emanating from behind one of the seemingly empty houses.

She wavered for a moment, weighing up her options.

She didn't have time to double-back and go around.

Night was closing in on her fast, and she decided that she would rather risk being spotted by the locals again, instead of blindly stumbling over a tripwire in the darkness if she took a different route.

Tightening the grip on her combat knife, she kept her eyes fixated on the house's open carport, switching her stride back to stealth.

Crouching down by the curb, she used the tall stalks of overgrown grass to screen her advance, stopping just short of the driveway.

The flickering light of a campfire in the house's backyard spilled out into the street, illuminating a thin trail of ruddy brown blood leading from the asphalt into the carport.

The scent of sizzling meat wafted on the evening breeze, and

Riley's mouth began to water – although she wouldn't admit to herself whether it was out of hunger or nausea.

Not unless she knew what the meat had come from.

Coiling herself into a sprinter's pose, she was preparing to dash over to the next tuft of overgrown grass, when a giant shadow leapt out across the carport.

She swallowed edgily as a pair of male voices floated up from the backyard.

"You think it's ready yet? I'm starving."

"I dunno. Looks like he needs a couple more minutes."

"You always say that. And then we end up eating charcoaled asshole."

"Do you wanna fucking cook him then?"

"Whatever. I'm gonna take a piss."

Pulse pounding in her ears, Riley peered in between the spears of grass as a young man with an athletic build rounded the corner, his sneakers scuffing the carport's concrete.

"You think we're getting any closer to finding the two girls?" he called back over his shoulder as he leaned up against the wooden fence.

"Must be," the second voice supposed. "I mean, who else would've shot this thing and just left him to die?"

That's my fucking hare, Riley realized, her eyes narrowing as the first guy sprang a leak.

The contents of her backpack shifted as she slowly drew herself upright, the soft rustle masked by the sound of his piss hitting the fence.

"Well, they're out there somewhere," he groaned heartily, throwing his head back and staring up at the stars in the night sky. "I feel like tomorrow's gonna be the day."

"Why not tonight?" Riley whispered into his ear. She clapped her gloved hand over his mouth, muffling his startled yelp as she pressed her combat knife against his throat. "Hands up. How many in your group?"

Jolting at the sharp edge of serrated teeth biting into his skin, he slowly raised his arms, holding up two shaky fingers while the rest of his stream splashed across his sneakers.

Two, Riley glanced over her shoulder.

She could handle two.

"Better be," she pulled him away from the fence, facing him towards the backyard. "Walk."

He tried to glance down at his feet, prompting a swift prick from the blade.

With the amount of adrenaline coursing through Riley's veins, if he so much as twitched the wrong way, she'd slash his throat from ear to ear purely on instinct.

Whimpering behind her gloved hand, he stepped falteringly towards the flickering firelight around the corner, his limp dick still dribbling droplets in between his sneakers.

Breathing shallow, Riley's sharp eyes scanned the backyard.

There was only one other person behind the house.

He was chubby, with shoulder-length curly blonde hair, and a backwards black baseball cap.

Bending over a rusty barbecue grill on a concrete slab in the middle of the yard, he had his back turned to their approach.

"Should be about done," he called over his shoulder, snapping his metal tongs in the air. "Bring that tray over here."

Riley's gaze flicked towards the pair of plates and cutlery on the outdoor dining table. Beside the metal tray were a cutting board and a kitchen knife, its bloodstained edge giving off a sinister sheen in the firelight.

"Oi, dickhead," he turned around. His jaw dropped at the

28

sight of Riley holding his buddy at knifepoint. He took a step back, almost knocking over the barbecue grill. "Oh shit, who the fuck are you!?"

"Put your hands above your head," Riley's eyes dropped to his waist, searching for a weapon. "Or Dickhead dies."

"What do you want?" the cook held up his hands, wincing as the meat began to char behind him. "Was this your kill? You can have it. I swear, we thought the cats killed him until we saw the bullet. They were already getting into him by the time we found him."

"Cut the shit," she spat, glaring at him icily. "I heard you guys talking. You're looking for two girls, right? Well, here's one. What now?"

The life in her hands tried to speak, his voice muffled against her glove.

"What? That was –" the cook gulped nervously, staring at the tip of her blade pressing into his buddy's neck. "We weren't talking about you. I swear – I fucking swear! We're just looking for our friends. Please, just let him go. We'll leave. You can have the meat. Just – fuck!!"

Riley's head cocked slightly, narrowing her eyes at the desperation on his face.

She wasn't convinced.

She had run into enough liars to know better than to trust her own ears.

Braxton Shepherd.

Sergeant Turnbull.

Even Calvin Fisher had more guile than this guy.

"Bullshit," Riley slit the surface of her hostage's skin, hard enough to draw blood, making sure that they knew she wasn't messing around. "Here's the real story. You came here to check

29

on your trap in that alley. Then you saw the blood on the ground, and you followed the trail back here to an easy dinner. There's nothing like a nice little meal to break up the hunt for a couple of girls, right?"

"What fucking trap?" his eyes fixated on the small trickle of blood weeping down his buddy's neck. The metal tongs rattled as his face twisted with anxiety, "What fucking alley? What — fucking — hunt are you talking about!?"

The meat on the grill blackened as Riley stared him down.

"Hey, you guys?" a high-pitched voice broke in from the other side of the carport. "It's me. I found those two girls you were looking for."

There's three of them, Riley thought to herself. *Fuck.*

Checking over her shoulder, she steered her hostage back towards the house until she was standing against the brick wall, ensuring that the new arrival couldn't blindside her.

"Dylan, don't come back here!" the baseball cap-wearing blonde yelled, before shooting a glance at his buddy and dropping his tone. "I dunno how the fuck he always finds us."

"It's pretty easy," Dylan's voice piped up again, his shoes scuffing the concrete driveway. "I just follow the smell of burnt food. What's for dinner, you guys?"

"Dylan, I'm telling you —"

A kid in a yellow shirt came around the corner.

The same kid who had gaped back at Riley and Heather from across the street.

The same kid who had run her ragged across town.

Riley's lips tightened into a cold smile, her suspicions confirmed.

"Oh," Dylan stopped in his tracks as soon as he caught sight of her, his face cringing at the sight of blood trickling down her hostage's neck. The kid's eyes dropped to his shoes as he pointed shakily, "T–t–that's her... I thought you said you guys were f–f–friends?"

"Get lost, kid," Riley hissed through gritted teeth, keeping her gaze locked on the amateur chef, his eyes sliding sideways towards the kitchen knife on the cutting board.

The other guy squirmed in her grip as he struggled to say something, one finger pointing at her gloved hand covering his mouth.

There was no point in keeping him quiet now.

She cupped his chin instead, roughly turning his head upwards to the night sky as her thirsty blade licked at his throat.

"Demi and Taylor!" he yelled, dancing on his tiptoes. Panting heavily, he elaborated, "We're looking for Demi and Taylor."

CHAPTER 8

"Which one of you is Jack?" Riley Armstrong tested, still holding her combat knife to the athletic guy's throat.

"How did you – well, I'm... Zack?" the man at her mercy stared up at the starry night sky, hoping that it was the answer she was looking for. He pointed at his blonde buddy standing beside the barbecue. "That's Austin."

On the road from Colorado, Heather had told her the names of the other scavengers from her group.

But including Taylor and Demi, there was only meant to be four of them.

"Why were you watching the house?" she turned to Dylan, the curly-haired kid still averting his gaze from the thin line of blood trickling down Zack's neck.

"They told me to," he answered timidly, his eyes fixed intently on the ground.

"We figured the girls might come back to Josh's house," Austin explained, his fearful eyes still on edge, even as his arms began to drop. "We told Dylan to keep an eye out for Heather as well – she's another one of our friends. I dunno what she's gonna do when we tell her we lost her sister, but she knows this town better than we do. I'm hoping she'll get here soon so she can help us look."

"It's Heather," Zack snorted at him, despite still standing on his tiptoes at Riley's mercy. "Of course she'll fucking look for her own sister."

Riley exhaled a shaky breath.

He knows their names, she heard her mother's voice in her ears, remembering when they had caught up to the carjackers outside Grandma Eleanor's house. *Shaun knew their names too*, she reminded herself. *Right before he tried to kill us.*

She kept the tip of her blade at Zack's throat.

Her sharp eyes flicked from Austin to Dylan.

Her questions were too easy.

She needed something solid to make sure that it was really Heather's group, and not some trio of pretenders who had murdered them on the road, adopting their names and story for themselves.

"Back in Kansas," Riley narrowed her eyes at Austin, "Heather kept her car in the garage. What was the color of her suburban?"

"*Suburban?*" Zack breathed in bewilderment, his life hanging on the answer to a trick question. "Heather had a yellow hatchback. Or it used to be yellow. It was old as fuck. I dunno. Whatever yellow looks like after the paint fades. Please don't fucking kill me!"

Satisfied, Riley pulled her blade and shoved him forward.

"Fucking hell," he spluttered, finally zipping up his fly before gingerly touching his neck. "How bad is it?"

"Looks better already," Austin tightened his lips as he glanced back at the burnt meat. "Hey, Dylan, grab me that tray."

"So, you're with Heather then," Zack eyed Riley as he stood beside the barbecue grill, wiping the blood from his throat and examining his fingers in the flickering firelight. "Fucking figures. You got a name?"

"Doesn't everybody?" she asked sarcastically, watching as Austin tossed the burnt meat into the metal tray. Still clenching her combat knife in her fist, she cast a wary glance around the corner, checking the street. "Look, if you guys didn't set up that trap in the alley, then we need to get moving before whoever did comes back."

*

CHAPTER 9

"YOU LOST MY FUCKING SISTER!?" Heather exploded out of the couch in the front room, before her wounded leg sent her reeling to the floor.

She snarled into the carpet as pale moonlight shone through the window.

Riley stooped to help her up, but the fiery redhead knocked her hand away.

Zack and Austin stood sheepishly out in the hallway, neither one of them wanting to set foot inside the room.

Dylan sat back in an armchair with the metal tray on his lap, his shoes dangling above the floor as he held Heather's share of the hare.

"We've been looking everywhere for – "

"Shut the fuck up, Austin. Shut – the fuck – up," Heather warned as she rose up on her good foot. A shadow crossed her face, and she locked eyes with Riley for an instant before glaring at her two friends again. "You know what? I could tell Riley here to cross you both the fuck out, and she'd do it. Right where you're standing. Don't look at the door, Zack. You wouldn't make it that far."

She sank down onto the couch again, cursing her injury underneath her breath.

"You want some food?" Riley was the first to break the silence.

"Yes, I want some food," Heather snapped, before taking a deep breath to recompose herself. "Thank you, Riley. Thank you – whatever your name is."

"Dylan," he flashed a toothy grin at her as he dropped off the delivery, happy to be free of the temptation.

"Looks like Demi's definitely gone," Heather remarked, picking up a charred piece of meat and popping it into her mouth all the same.

The sound of her chewing seemed to reverberate in the stillness.

Her rigid shoulders slackened as she savored the gamy flavor, reaching for another.

Riley stifled a smirk, realizing that Heather had just been hangry.

She had no doubt in her mind that the woman was pissed about her missing sister, but their steady diet of cat biscuits over the past few days certainly hadn't done wonders for her mood.

"Where's Dwayne at?" Zack asked, glancing down the dark hall towards the kitchen.

"Dead," Riley replied casually, eyeing both of them.

"Fuck," Austin's gaze fell to the floor, searching the carpet for words.

"How'd he die?" Zack looked from Heather to Riley.

"Quick," Riley shrugged, remembering the school's storage shed at Leadthorne High, and how Dwayne had threatened to sever her spinal cord, leaving her paralyzed from the neck down.

"Not the way I would've done it."

"He was our friend, you piece of –"

"So, are you guys gonna tell me what happened here?" Heather asked around another mouthful, taking on her usual tone of nonchalance again.

Austin seethed at Riley, readjusting his black baseball cap before glancing sidelong at Zack, silently volunteering him to explain.

"Your cousin was long gone by the time we got here," Zack stepped into the room, reeling off the same story that they had told Riley on their way back to the house. He gazed down at Heather with one hand in his pocket, "We knew we had to wait for you though, so after we checked the strip mall, we split up to search the area for supplies. We did it just like we always do. Same way we did it back home. And the same way we did it when we were out on the road. But the day we got here was the last time we saw either of them."

"That's what happened to me and Nancy too," Dylan chimed in from his oversized armchair. "She's my big sister. One day, she went out looking for fuel, and then she never came back. But maybe if we can find your guys's friends, we can find Nancy too."

"How long's she been missing?" Heather had her eyes on Zack.

"I'm not sure how many weeks or months it's been now," Dylan took the question that wasn't meant for him. He smiled wearily, more to himself than anyone else, "But I still haven't given up hope yet."

Riley and Heather exchanged a knowing glance.

His big sister was probably dead by now.

"The girls haven't been gone for that long," Austin reassured

37

Heather from the hall.

Zack cocked an eyebrow at him before going over to the window.

"How long?" Riley asked, her gaze switching between the two.

They hadn't told her that part yet.

Heather's striking green eyes were laser-focused on Austin.

"Six...teen days," he wilted under her frosty glare, "Seventeen tomorrow."

Fuming, the fiery redhead flexed her fingers before balling her hand into a fist.

"Who's the piece of shit now?" Riley asked, drilling her gaze into Austin. She looked over at Heather, with one hand straying towards the combat knife strapped to her thigh. "Hey, if you want, I don't mind getting my blade wet. It'll be one less mouth for us to feed."

She didn't mean it.

But from the panicked expression on Austin's face, he believed her.

"What about that one guy living out on the edge of town?" Zack suggested, turning away from the window. "Think we should try asking him again?"

"Yeah, it's worth a shot!" Austin eagerly latched on to the change of subject. His eyes lingered on Heather's white-knuckled fist before turning to Riley. "You girls might have a better chance at talking to him. He doesn't wanna talk to us. But maybe he knows something we don't."

"That's a low bar to beat," Riley gave a small snort, sharing half a smirk with Heather. "Alright, how do we find this guy?"

"His place is pretty hard to miss," Dylan stared down at his shoes dangling over the floor. "I don't go out that way anymore.

You'll see why when you get there."

CHAPTER 10

Dylan checked back over his shoulder to make sure that they were still behind him.

"How much farther is this place?" Riley called ahead, shading her eyes against the mid-morning sun.

"Beats me," Zack grunted as he walked beside her, the cowlick at the back of his messy brown hair rising and falling with every step. "This is the first time he's ever mentioned having somewhere else to hang out – other than wherever we happen to be."

"Come on, you guys, we're nearly there!" Dylan walked sideways as he looked over his shoulder, waiting for them to catch up to the next intersection before he turned the corner.

"Looks like this town didn't waste any time when they heard the news," Heather remarked while Austin pushed her office chair from behind, all of them gazing at the supermarket's parking lot on the other side of the intersection.

Decomposing corpses and sun-bleached skeletons were sprawled across the concrete no-man's-land, dismembered by packs of wild animals that had played macabre games of tug-of-war.

Shopping carts were scattered and overturned, their woeful wheels slowly turning with the wind. Some of them lay beside the open trunks of bullet-riddled suburbans and station wagons, along with the dead panic shoppers who hadn't been fast enough to load up their supplies before being gunned down from behind.

Riley remembered the supermarket back in Redhurst, when she and her father had lost their slabs of bottled water to the frenzied crowd. She wondered whether its parking lot looked any different from the one in this town, especially once the shelves had gotten scarce.

Passing by the scorched shells of police vehicles along the avenue, they soon turned into a side street, backpacks rustling on their shoulders.

Following the road's curve through the silent neighborhood, Dylan finally stopped at the mouth of a cul-de-sac.

"We're here," he announced, turning to flash them all a toothy grin, before pointing up at a double-story house on the corner.

The property sat a few feet above the street level, so it had been ringed by a stone retaining wall. But other than that, it just looked like another regular weatherboard home that had been abandoned after the apocalypse.

With its untended garden beds, closed curtains and dead pot plants lining the veranda, there was nothing special about the place that set it apart from any other house. Only the most thorough of scavengers would have thought to search for supplies here.

But that was probably the exact same reason why Dylan and his sister had chosen it.

"I know it doesn't look like much," he chirped happily,

climbing the retaining wall's steps and bouncing up the garden path towards the veranda. "But wait until you guys see what's inside!"

"We're gonna go around," Austin declared from behind Heather, pushing her office chair towards the driveway in the neck of the cul-de-sac.

"Oh, okay," the curly-haired kid mumbled as he remembered Heather's injured leg. He looked over at the veranda's steps skeptically, before changing direction. "Well, we don't have to go in through the front door anyway."

Riley and Zack shared a sidelong glance before following him towards the downward-sloping driveway.

Climbing up onto one of the trash bins parked beside the house's big wooden gate, Dylan hoisted himself up and over the fence, grunting softly as he dropped down on the other side.

He unlocked the gate's latch with a *clack*, and the driveway's double doors swung open.

"Makes you wonder how the owners used to open it," Heather pondered in her chair, her boot heel skidding along the concrete as Austin trundled her down the sloping driveway.

"Well, if they had a gate that only opened with a remote," Riley spoke over her shoulder with half a smirk, "You'd be hopping up the front steps right about now."

"Fuck you," Heather snorted with a twitch of her eyebrows.

A decrepit old sedan greeted them from the bottom of the hill, housed in an open carport. It was nestled between a rusty shed and the house's back entrance, where a weather-beaten shopping cart stood.

"Are you guys ready to be blown away?" Dylan beamed back at them with his hand on the door handle, unable to contain his excitement.

"Not if there's a shotgun waiting on the other side," Zack quipped, stooping to help Austin lift Heather's chair up onto the back step.

"Come on, you guys, I wouldn't do that to my friends," Dylan threw the door open and stepped aside. He smiled up at Riley before bowing with an exaggerated hand gesture, "Ladies first."

She shook her head with a chuckle before stepping inside.

The house's back entrance led into an L-shaped basement, with a wooden staircase set along the wall in the center of the room. A pair of small rectangular windows on the other end allowed some sunlight in, but the front garden's overgrown shrubs cast deep shadows across the floor.

"No – fucking – way," she could barely believe her eyes.

"Damn, kid, you've been holding out on us!" Zack pushed past Riley as he made a beeline for the shelves.

Half of the basement's wall was lined with canned soup, fruit preserves, jars of honey and peanut butter. Sacks of rice, sugar and flour occupied the bottom shelves, while the entire top half of one rack had been dedicated to cartons of long-life milk, along with plastic containers brimming with packets of instant coffee.

"Riley, are you done gawking yet?" Heather kicked the back of her leg before a gasp escaped her lips, her eyes snapping towards the shelves.

Austin left her chair spinning in the doorway as he joined Zack, both of them unshouldering their backpacks and loading up on whatever they could carry.

"Check this out," Zack tossed him a can of baked beans. "I haven't seen these in ages."

"I hope this place has some good ventilation," Austin chortled, cracking open the can and slurping the beans down cold.

43

"How the hell did you get all this by yourself?" Riley was still looking around the room as she walked over to the shelves.

An old floral-print couch had been pushed underneath the staircase, along with a wooden table, making room for a pair of mattresses where Dylan and his sister had probably slept. In the other corner of the room was a camping stove sitting on top of a waist-high cabinet.

"I didn't," Dylan filed in after Heather, his eyes going over to Zack and Austin uncertainly as they filled up their backpacks. "It was already like this when me and Nancy got here. She was picking some herbs from the garden, and then she saw the shelves through one of the windows."

"Are those herbs still up there?" Riley asked as she unzipped her backpack and went to work, grabbing cans of tomatoes and peaches.

"We already ate them all, back when we had gas to cook with," Dylan replied, watching with slumped shoulders as the three of them raided the shelves. His eyes dropped to his feet. "She told me not to tell anybody about this place."

"Your sister sounds like a smart girl," Heather placed a gentle hand on his arm. "There are some bad people out there who would point a gun at you for half of what you've got in here."

Riley paused for a moment, glancing over her shoulder to see Heather staring back at her with raised eyebrows, bitterly reminding her exactly how the two of them had met.

"You guys aren't just gonna take all the food and leave, are you?" Dylan's eyes searched the floor, wondering if he had made a mistake by bringing them here.

"We're not going anywhere," Riley reassured him, glancing at the guilt of impulse on the others' faces. She zipped up her backpack again and swung it over her shoulder, the extra weight an unfamiliar but welcome burden. "We're just keeping it safe. You don't wanna keep all your food in the one place, right?"

"Well, no – I didn't even think about that," he breathed a sigh of relief, color soon filling his cheeks again. He looked over at Zack and Austin as they turned away from the shelves. "Sorry I didn't bring you guys here sooner. But after last night, I just thought – if you guys spent less time looking for food, then we'd have more time to look for my sister. Oh, and your guys's friends too. And now that there's five of us, we should be able to find them a lot faster!"

"You can count me out – I won't be able to help," Heather admitted with a sullen gaze. "Not with my leg like this. I'd only slow you down."

"Come on over to the light," Zack jerked his head towards the two windows on the other side of the basement. "That bandage needs changing. Let's have a look at what you've gone and done to yourself. Austin, you know where to look."

"Bathrooms and linen closet," he nodded as he set foot on the wooden staircase.

"You don't wanna go up there," Dylan warned, taking two quick steps towards the stairs. "The first level's okay. But Nancy said there's a dead guy in one of the bedrooms."

"So?" Austin frowned with an amused grin. "Did you not see the parking lot on the way here? I'm waiting for the day that we *don't* find a dead body."

"You better hope that day comes soon," Heather's voice filled the basement as she glowered around the room. "Because if you don't come back with my sister – alive – I'm gonna be sending one of you to keep her company."

Her menacing green gaze settled on Riley.

CHAPTER 11

"Dude, check this out," Austin's footsteps drummed back down the wooden staircase, cradling a duffel bag brimming with medical supplies. "Guy's got a bunch of bug-out bags up in his closet."

"Yeah, no guns though," Riley Armstrong followed him back into the basement with an armful of linen. She furrowed her eyebrows, staring at the shelves lining the wall. "Who the hell stocks up on all these supplies, and doesn't even think to at least have something to defend it all with?"

"I'm guessing that's how he died?" Zack supposed, rummaging through the duffel bag until he found a pair of scissors.

"Guess again," Riley set the pile of linen down on the old floral-print couch underneath the stairs, glancing down at the dingy pair of mattresses before rounding the corner again.

"There'd be nothing left down here if the house got raided," Heather knew, wincing on the floor as Zack began cutting through the bloody crust of her makeshift bandage.

"Dickhead died reaching for a bottle of pills on his night-stand," Austin chortled, shaking his head at the irony. "Imagine having almost everything you'd need to ride out the apocalypse, and this guy probably died of a fucking heart attack before it even started."

Heather grunted in pain as Zack peeled the soaked sanitary pad from her wound.

"Damn, I dunno whether to say you ran outta luck or you lucked out," he studied her leg closely before flinging the old bandage at Austin's feet. "One inch to the left and you'd be *screaming* right now. One inch to the right and you'd be having a good day."

"Just fix it," she huffed, lying back and staring up at the ceiling, bracing herself against the approaching agony.

Zack began plucking bloodstained fibers of fabric from her wound with a pair of tweezers, while Heather's sharp hisses of pain cursed each one's removal.

"How about you go and change those bed sheets?" Riley shot an authoritative glance at Austin before taking a seat on Heather's office chair. "Where's the kid, anyway?"

Austin scowled at Riley for a moment, with sour words on his lips, when he took another look at Heather's wound. Promptly swallowing his reply, he disappeared around the corner.

"I sent him to get some – fucking hell, Zack – firewood," Heather answered, her gaze meeting Riley's, trying to take her mind off the searing stings. She nodded towards the plastic containers on the shelves, "I'm gonna have a bucket-sized cup of coffee after this shit."

"And then what?" Riley leaned over her, but not for the sake of keeping the conversation going.

"Then, you're gonna bring back Taylor and Demi," she screwed her eyes shut as Zack poured water over her wound.

"And then what?" Riley pressed, patiently waiting for her to catch on.

"Then, we're gonna stay here until my leg heals up and all the food's gone," Heather snapped open her eyelids and stared up at Riley.

"And – then – what?" she repeated relentlessly.

"You really wanna talk about this now?" Heather bristled at the interrogation before looking over at Zack. "What the hell's taking you so long?"

"Oh, I'm sorry, I'm just making sure you don't lose your leg to an infection," his eyes were focused on pouring a jar of honey onto a new dressing. "You're welcome, by the way."

Austin chuckled from around the corner.

"What the hell, Zack!?" her eyes flitted to the duffel bag lying on the floor out of reach. "Isn't there any antiseptic in there?"

"There probably is," he shrugged, setting aside the dressing before leaning his weight down onto her thigh, clamping her leg to the floor while holding the jar of honey aloft. "Trust me though. This'll work better. Don't move now."

"*Do not tip that jar!*" Heather growled through gritted teeth. She shot upright, grabbing his arm before he could pour the honey onto her wound. "Riley, get the medicine. Don't let this idiot fuck up my leg any worse – not over some home remedy hippie bullshit!"

For a woman who had threatened to kill one of them only ten minutes ago, she was certainly proving how much she really needed them.

"Not until you answer my question," Riley's head cocked slightly, still waiting for an answer.

"Fine – fuck it!" Heather yelled as she wrestled with Zack's arm. "If you bring back Taylor and Demi, we'll all go with you to Redhurst. But I'm gonna need both of my legs if we're gonna make it there!"

"That's all I needed to hear," she smiled victoriously before turning to Zack. "What the hell's wrong with you? Give her some damn antiseptic like a normal person."

"Alright," he backed off with a resigned sigh, screwing the lid back on the jar of honey. "This is antiseptic, antibiotics and antioxidants all in one. But have it your way."

"Whether it would've worked or not doesn't matter," Riley replied as he turned to rummage through the duffel bag. "We can eat honey. We can't eat medicine."

"Neither could that guy upstairs," Austin laughed again from around the corner.

Zack held up a pair of bottles in the light streaming in through the basement windows, twisting his lips as he studied the two labels.

Heather shook her head at both of her friends before signaling for Riley to come closer.

"You're the only one who can bring her back safe," Heather whispered into Riley's ear as she crouched beside the wounded woman. "These two... they're okay. But they're not you. Find my sister, Riley, and we'll have your back wherever you wanna go. Just watch your step out there."

CHAPTER 12

The midday spring sun beat down on the backs of their necks as the trio marched in mutual silence, heading along the pothole-scarred highway towards the outskirts of town.

Riley turned up the collar of her brown plaid shirt to shield her neck from the sun, but with little effect. Now that the weather was warming up again, she needed to find some more suitable clothes that could cope with the heat, especially since once they found the three missing girls, she and her new allies would be crossing through Nevada to get to California.

And from the state of the world these days, there was no guarantee that they'd be able to get a vehicle running either, let alone find enough fuel along the way to keep it going.

"I'm not asking her," Zack's low mutter to Austin from up ahead drifted back to Riley.

She was trailing behind the other two.

Partly because they were still strangers to her, having only met them last night.

But she was mostly keeping her distance in case they triggered another hidden trap.

"Well, don't look at me," Austin snorted, elbowing him in

the ribs as they walked. "You're the one who wants to know."

"She had a fucking knife to my throat," Zack whispered back. "I'm not risking that again. Forget I said anything. We'll probably find out soon enough anyway."

"Find out what?" Riley called ahead, mildly intrigued.

"Shit," Zack cursed under his breath. He glanced over his shoulder, making eye contact with her for a fleeting moment, before turning his eyes back to the road again.

Austin sniggered beside him as a forest rose up on one side of the highway.

"Well..." Zack thrust his hands into his pockets. "We were wondering –"

"*You* were wondering," Austin corrected him.

"Are you a good cook?" Zack blurted it out, like ripping off a bandage, but he refused to look back at her this time.

Riley smirked to herself as she decided to make him sweat a little, leaving his question hanging in the air for an uncomfortable length of time.

"No," she finally gave him an answer, to his visible relief, his shoulders relaxing. "I mean, I can start a fire, throw some shit together into a pan, and wait for it to stop being raw. But that doesn't mean it'll taste any good."

"Well, I hope we find the girls soon then," Zack sighed as the buildings on the other side of the highway grew fewer and farther between. "I haven't had a decent meal in weeks."

"Thanks, dickhead," Austin stared sidelong at him before shaking his head with a huff. "You fucking cook tonight then."

"Well, hold on – Demi was a chef," Zack spluttered out his explanation, before turning back to face Riley. "Like, a proper chef. She used to work in the kitchen at a golf course's clubhouse near our neighborhood – real classy restaurant. I

51

think. I never ate there myself. But with the way she cooks, it *had* to be classy."

"Yeah, I miss her too," Austin admitted as he kicked a rock down the middle of the highway. "Not just for her cooking either, but she's pretty damn good at it. That hare last night – she could've made that meat melt in your mouth."

Just as Riley's taste buds were beginning to water, she had to suppress the urge to gag.

The telltale stench of long-dead corpses rotting in the sun pervaded her nostrils.

At this point in the post-apocalypse, she didn't need to cover her nose anymore.

But she did have to swallow her excess saliva in order to avoid retching at the sight.

Dozens of decomposing bodies lay in a ditch along one side of the highway, opposite the forest, filling the space in between the road and a barbed wire fence.

Knee-high rocks and boulders lined both edges of the dreadful ditch, along with one pickup truck that had unsuccessfully tried to bulldoze its way through the barricade.

Rusty tin cans hung from each fence post, interspersed with several warning signs that very clearly stated – one way or another – *No Trespassing*.

As if a ditch full of corpses isn't enough of a warning, Riley shook her head, wondering how many raiders had taken their chances anyway.

But then again, maybe most of these people had tried to enter from a different side of the property.

Her arms budded with gooseflesh as her mind's eye flashed back to Wyoming, where her old group had unknowingly trespassed on somebody else's land. She and her mother had stood shaking outside a nightmarish shed, while Clarence, the leopard-print panties-wearing drug addict, had violently accused them of ignoring his non-existent warning sign.

But these signs were very real.

And whoever lived here was just as dangerous – if not more so.

No wonder Dylan stopped coming out this way, Riley thought to herself in complete comprehension.

She peered into the sea of overgrown grass swaying across the front of the big sloping property, the twin fields of green on either side of the gravel driveway stretching up over a hill and disappearing behind the crest.

"Riley, over here," Zack beckoned for her to come closer to where he and Austin were standing.

A strikingly different sign hung from the gravel driveway's gatepost.

Pull cord for trading inquiries.

"Is this guy serious?" Riley furrowed her eyebrows in disbelief.

Her gaze went from the row of dead bodies to a wooden shelf mounted underneath the sign, where a length of paracord hung beside a landline phone's handset.

An electrical cable sprouted from the base of the handset, traveling in unison with the paracord up one side of the driveway and over the hill in the distance.

"Take a good look at that ditch and tell me he's not serious," Austin snorted as he gave the cord a quick tug. Then, offering Riley the phone, he added, "Good luck."

CHAPTER 13

Riley held the phone's receiver to her ear, while scanning the hill's ridgeline for any signs of movement.

Shackled in place by her own grip around the phone, and with the woods at her back, she couldn't help but feel like she was in the perfect position for a predator to pounce.

Having Zack and Austin to watch her back didn't do anything to soothe her nerves either – not from the way that their shoes were scuffing the asphalt behind her, the pair of them edgily pacing back and forth with bated breaths.

Riley rubbed the back of her neck with her gloved hand, shifting her weight with unease.

She was just about to hang up the phone, when a *click* sounded from the other side.

"What do you have?" a rough voice rasped through the landline.

Riley jerked the receiver's jolt of static away from her ear – the sharp crackle either owing to the man's brusque tone of voice, or the phone's tinny-pitched speaker.

"Peaches," she replied with reserve, her answer almost sounding like a question in response. She stared at the phone's cable running the length of the gravel driveway and up over the hill, wondering if he had even heard her. Summoning her voice – louder this time – she tried again, "Canned peaches and tomatoes."

"We've already got food," he shot back, "Better than that shit in a tin. What else?"

Riley glanced back over her shoulder at Zack and Austin, trying to remember what they had taken from the shelves in the basement.

But the only thing that came to mind was the image of Austin slurping down a cold can of baked beans.

"How about you tell us what you want?" she furrowed her eyebrows at the ridgeline. "We can get it for you."

"*You can get it for me*," he echoed with a mix of skepticism and disdain. "Here's an idea. How about you run along and bring back Football Sundays? Then we'll talk."

Riley clenched the phone in her fist, but she let him have his little moment of bitter longing.

She remembered how prickly Virge Norton had been the first day she met him – and every day after.

"I don't think you have anything we need," the man on the other end of the phone decided abruptly. "We've already got everything we could ask for, and if you had anything better than cans of fucking peaches, you would've led with that instead."

"I like peaches," a woman's voice piped up in the background. "Who's that on the phone, Everett?"

"Rose, I told y–"

Another wave of static sounded through the speaker as a hand clapped over the phone.

Riley blocked her other ear, straining to hear the muffled conversation on the other end.

"Thank you," the woman's voice came again, closer this time. A faint rustle sounded as she lifted the phone to her ear. "You'll have to excuse my husband. He treats everybody like they're the enemy. Sometimes, I don't know why we even bothered to put up that sign. What's your name, sweetie?"

"Riley," she answered after a few seconds of silence, disarmed by the married couple's polar opposites in personality.

"Well, Riley, I'm Rose," she replied with a happy sigh.

Riley could feel her lips curling into a slight smile, the pair of women sharing a mutual moment of nostalgia – over something as simple as a friendly voice on the other end of a phone call.

"We'd love to have some peaches in our pantry again," Rose continued, her husband letting out a resigned grunt in the background. "But what can we offer you in return? We've got fish here, *plenty* of blackberries, and if you've got a thirst for something fresh, I just finished up on making a batch of carrot juice."

"We were actually just hoping for some information," Riley looked back over her shoulder at Zack and Austin's stunned faces, evidently having made it further in conversation than either of them had been able to. "We're looking for a few of our friends. They went missing a couple of weeks ago, and we were hoping that you guys might have some ideas on where to look."

"Sure, we'll do what we can to help you," Rose replied, before drawing in a sharp breath, her voice fading. "Oh, Everett, put that away. Hey, I mean it. She's not trespassing if I'm inviting her in. *Everett!*"

Riley bit her bottom lip, listening to the sounds of heavy footfalls and a door slamming.

Pulse pounding, her eyes slid sideways to the row of bodies

lying dead in the ditch.

Snapping her gaze towards the trees on the other side of the highway, she jabbed a finger at the forest, mouthing silently at Zack and Austin to hide in the woods.

A clanging cowbell rang from somewhere over the hill, and Riley dropped the phone, turning to follow the two guys, when the other end of the dangling landline rustled again.

"Riley, sweetie, are you still there?" Rose's voice came back, still trying to be soft and soothing, but audibly taut with tension now. "Don't mind Everett. He gets a little bit overprotective of me sometimes. I can promise you though – he's just a big old teddy bear. Let him do his thing, and we'll talk about your friends over some fresh carrot juice, okay?"

Heart hammering in her chest, Riley stared up at the hill's ridgeline.

She felt as though a gigantic pair of magnets were threatening to tear her in half.

On one hand, she could accept Rose's invitation, walk up the gravel driveway, and roll the dice on whether Everett would shoot her for daring to set foot on his property.

But on the other hand, if she hid in the forest with Zack and Austin, they would lose this opportunity to have a few locals on their side. The three of them would wander around the town, aimlessly searching for Taylor, Demi and Nancy, until Heather finally made good on her death threats.

Either way, it was a gamble, and Riley knew that dithering with her indecision wasn't going to make any difference.

Especially since – judging from the flash on the hilltop – Everett already had her in his sights.

CHAPTER 14

"Hang up the phone and open the gate!" Everett's orders boomed from the top of the hill. "Do it now – do it slow!!"

Flexing her gloved fingers to summon her resolve, Riley Armstrong placed the dangling phone back into its cradle, before slowly unlatching the gate and pushing it open.

CRASH!

Riley's heart leapt up into her throat.

Jolting backwards, she checked herself to see if she had been hit by something.

An old metal bucket filled with rocks had fallen to the ground beside the gate.

"Show me your hands!" Everett yelled from the ridgeline. "Show me your fucking hands!!"

Riley breathed out her jittery nerves, slowly raising her arms.

She didn't dare glance back over her shoulder as she stepped through the gate, not wanting to give away Zack and Austin's position in the forest – as if they could do anything to help her anyway.

The gate swung shut behind her, setting off a series of rattles from the rusty tin cans hanging all along the property's barbed wire fence.

"Let's go, Riley!" Everett shouted from behind the glint on the hilltop, "Keep walking!"

Taking a galvanizing breath, she focused on putting one foot in front of the other, her gaze dropping to the upward-sloping gravel driveway.

In her peripheral vision – past the hanging lengths of paracord and the landline phone's electrical cable – she could see flashes of metal lying scattered in the swaying sea of overgrown grass.

Just in case the barbed wire fence doesn't work, she supposed, beginning to admire the amount of work that the married couple had put into defending their home.

The tall stalks of grass had been cut back about a dozen yards from the ridgeline, where a small trench had been dug into the other side, providing plenty of cover against any frontal assaults.

It was there that she found Everett – a big brawny bear of a man – crouched behind the ridgeline with the barrel of an assault rifle pointed squarely at her chest.

"Leave the backpack on the ground," he growled, nodding towards the trench continuing on the other side of the gravel driveway. "Any weapons too. Toss them."

Riley held his penetrating gaze for a moment.

They were both strangers to each other.

But this was his property.

And he was just being cautious.

Best welcome anyone can hope for these days, Hayden Marsh's voice echoed in her ears.

Relenting with a sigh, Riley shrugged off her backpack.

Lifting the hem of her brown plaid shirt next, she slowly drew her pistol from the waistband of her jeans at the small of her back, tossing the empty handgun beside her pack.

"Blade goes too," Everett glanced pointedly at the combat knife strapped to her thigh. "Then empty out your pockets."

"No, I'm not giving up my knife," Riley snorted at the request, pulling out nothing but clumps of lint from her pockets.

"Turn around and fuck off then," he glowered up at her, his weathered face hardening. "You're not getting anywhere near my wife with that on you."

She could see the man's savagery simmering just beneath the surface.

There was a certain level of ruthlessness required to slaughter dozens of raiders, leaving them all lying dead in a ditch to rot in the sun – yet still possessing enough self-restraint to hold his fire, so that his wife could win herself a few cans of peaches for her pantry.

Riley had no doubt about how brutal the man could be.

Narrowing her eyes at Everett, against her better judgment, she drew her combat knife and threw it down at his feet, silently hoping that the serrated edge would stick in the dirt in between his boots.

It didn't.

Despite the aggressiveness of having a knife thrown at his feet, the severity in his stare subsided, and the barrel of his gun drifted off-center.

"Alright, now lift up your jeans," his frown remained rigid as he studied her ankles. "Show me your waist. Turn around."

"Are you done gawking yet?" Riley cocked an eyebrow at him, folding the hem of her shirt back down again.

"One last thing," Everett grunted as he climbed to his feet. He combed the whiskers of his stubbled beard, shooting a sidelong glance at the front windows of his house in the distance. "Hold still for a second."

He held his assault rifle in one hand, pointing the barrel towards the ground as he approached her, his other arm outstretched.

Riley retreated half a step as the back of his hand brushed down one side of her navel.

She already knew what was coming next as he frisked the other side.

Holding her breath with a frosty glare into his downcast gaze, she stood motionless as he tapped two knuckles against the fabric around her chest.

"That's it, you're good," Everett's hand flinched back as if he had been reaching into a fire. "Head on down, I'll grab your gear," his rough voice was already beginning to soften. "It's been a long time since Rose has had any visitors so... do me a favor and don't be a dick."

Riley's thumbs went to her shoulders to adjust the straps of her backpack that was no longer there. Feeling out of her element as Everett stooped to gather up her possessions, she crossed her arms across her chest instead, marching down the hill towards another barricade of sorts.

A sprawling ring of tall dense blackberry bushes had been planted around the married couple's modest wooden house and their small lake – probably serving as an internal perimeter, just in case any raiders could manage to breach the outer defenses.

Blocking the gravel driveway was a big iron-barred gate, towering above Riley.

She slowed her pace, suddenly overcome with a feeling of dread as she craned her neck, peering up at the row of spikes adorning the gate's top rail.

"You know what," she paused beside the gate's latch, turning back to face Everett. "I think I might take a rain check on that carrot juice. I'm happy for us to just talk and trade through the fence."

"Fine by me," he shrugged, carrying her backpack and weapons in one hand, and his assault rifle in the other. "I'll let Rose know. But you're not getting your shit back until you're on your way out."

Everett pushed through the gate, a cowbell clanging its greeting overhead.

Through the gate's iron bars and the spreading boughs of a solitary pinyon pine tree, Riley could see a lithe woman with tousled light brown hair sitting on the veranda, waving back at her.

"Hey, Riley, are you coming up?" Rose called across the distance, tilting her head slightly, with two glasses of carrot juice standing on a table beside her.

"She said she wants you to go to her," Everett answered, his head turning towards a set of fishing rods planted beside the lake. "Hey, I think we've got a bite!"

He left the gravel driveway to veer off towards his fishing poles.

"Oh, is everything okay?" Rose stood, climbing down the veranda's steps, making it halfway across the yard before remembering to grab the pair of glasses.

Biting her bottom lip, Riley's gaze went from Everett wrestling with a freshly-caught fish to Rose turning around with the glasses of carrot juice.

They were just a regular married couple trying to get by in the post-apocalypse.

Oddly enough, Riley could see glimpses of her own parents in

Rose and Everett.

If her father had survived the chaos of the road to Nebraska, she had no doubt that her family would still be living together at her Grandma Eleanor's house, enjoying the simple life, exactly like this – Nolan Armstrong suspicious of strangers, and Susan happily welcoming them in.

"What the hell am I doing?" Riley muttered under her breath before opening up the gate and stepping through. She held up a hand and called across to Rose, "Never mind, I'll come to you."

The cowbell rang again as the gate swung shut behind her.

"Well, I'm glad you changed your mind," Rose sighed with a smile from the shade of the veranda, sitting down in her chair again. "That sun sure is heating up out there."

Following the gravel driveway, Riley's hiking boots crunched over fallen leaves and brush as she passed by the pinyon pine tree.

She was returning Rose's smile, when her foot snagged on something.

Then, it was as if all the air in Riley's lungs had been sucked out.

A wooden clatter sounded from behind the tree trunk.

Lengths of rope zipped along the overhead branches.

A vortex of debris flew up all around her.

Pupils dilating, Riley's forearms instinctively shot up to shield her face.

Blinded by her own arms, she stumbled as the ground shifted.

Her knees buckling, she felt weightless, and her entire body was lifted up into the air.

CHAPTER 15

"WHAT THE FUCK!?" Riley roared the moment she could suck the breath back into her lungs.

Suspended above the gravel driveway, she was wrapped in the tight embrace of a heavy-duty fishing net, its tough nylon cords digging into the fabric of her clothes.

Snarling like a wild animal caught in a cage, she pulled her arms towards her chest, grabbed the closest hunk of mesh with her gloved hands, and *pulled*.

Nothing.

The diamond loops stretched, but that only served to tighten the knots in between.

Grunting with exertion, she couldn't rip the net apart – no matter how hard she tried.

"Yeah, we've definitely got a bite," Everett scorned as he stalked towards her from the lake.

Struggling in the snare, Riley cursed herself for giving up her knife.

But if the past nine months had taught her anything about herself – it was that she didn't need a weapon.

She was the weapon.

Glaring balefully at her approaching would-be captor, she clenched thick handfuls of the fishing net, drew the heels of her hiking boots underneath her, and *pushed.*

With the world mottled in mesh, there was no way to tell whether she was making any progress.

But she was determined not to end up like one of those bodies rotting in the ditch beside the highway.

She leaned forward, her face pressing up against the tough nylon cords, forcing her legs downwards with all her strength.

A guttural roar escaped from her gritted teeth as the bottom of the net finally tore open, and one of her boots plunged through the hole.

"Rose, get the bucket!" Everett yelled over his shoulder as he broke into a run.

An icy spike of adrenaline coursed through Riley's veins, and her gloved fingers scrabbled for the edges around the hole to rip the opening wider.

The whole net wobbled and warped as she wrenched and yanked, the snare spinning and swaying with every frenzied pull, her freed foot barely even touching the ground.

Just as she managed to snap another nylon cord, Everett tackled her leg, and the whole net swung sideways.

"Get the fuck off me, you lying piece of shit!" she shouted, kicking and twisting wildly in midair.

Hugging her leg to his chest with one brawny arm, Everett pulled off her boot with a stubborn *thock.*

Next, he peeled off her sweat-stained sock, wrinkling his nose up at her with a victorious grin.

"At what point did I lie?" he wondered aloud before climbing to his feet, still cradling her writhing leg in the crook of his elbow.

With Riley's entire body turned on an angle, Everett tossed her boot and sock beside the base of the pinyon pine tree's trunk.

She twisted and squirmed in the net.

None of it made any sense.

They already had her supplies.

Why put on the act after they already had my backpack? Riley turned the thought over in her mind.

They were a married couple – Everett had been hesitant to even frisk her – so it couldn't have been for *that* reason either.

And they have fish and carrots, so they can't be cannibals, she thought to herself – or rather, she hoped.

A chorus of wind chimes rang as Rose emerged from the house carrying a rusty bucket. She hurried down the veranda's stairs towards their entangled victim, the metal container's contents jangling with every step.

"What the hell do you want from me!?" Riley went still as she squinted at the bucket, trying to discern what was inside as it twinkled in the sun.

"Right now, we don't want you going anywhere," Everett growled as he gestured for his wife to come closer. "You're good, Rose. I've got her."

"I'm sorry, sweetie," Rose spoke softly as she tilted the bucket, shaking out shards of broken glass across the gravel driveway underneath the net. "From the moment I heard your voice, I knew I had to meet you in person. Our homemade landline tends to distort the sound a little, but..." she turned towards her husband, sighing with a glad smile. "She's perfect. I think she'll do just nicely."

CHAPTER 16

"I don't get it," Riley Armstrong furrowed her eyebrows in confusion, her gaze shifting between her two captors, "Perfect for what?"

"Your voice is just so full of emotion," Rose's eyes twinkled speculatively as she gazed up at her with a smile.

"Of course it's full of fucking emotion," Riley spat, struggling against Everett as he held her leg steady. "You lured me into a fucking fishing net, you crazy bitch!"

"Would you rather be lying dead in that ditch outside?" Everett growled menacingly. "Given where you are, I'm not gonna ask you to apologize. But I'm only gonna tell you once – watch your fucking mouth when you're talking to my wife."

Riley's tongue pressed against the inside of her cheek as she snorted at the audacity of his request.

"We won't keep you up there for too long – I promise," Rose reassured her, even as she emptied out the last of the glass shards underneath the snare. She turned to her husband, "Everett, could you fetch my chair from the veranda?"

"Sure thing – watch your foot," he glanced up at Riley, easing her leg down before marching towards the house.

Riley's bare foot brushed over a glass crystal, and she jerked her leg up from the ground.

"I want you to know that we weren't always like this," Rose tightened her lips, searching for the right words, as if she actually cared about what other people would think of the married couple's fall from grace. "We used to be just like every other family. We paid our taxes. Went out on date nights when we could. We worked hard for what we – "

"So did everybody else," Riley cut her off angrily. "You're not the only people in the world who got dealt a shit hand. We're all just trying to survive in this hell we're living in now."

"Yes, but once you have the food, the water, the shelter..." Rose nodded her thanks to Everett as he returned with her chair. "When you're not struggling to survive anymore, your mind starts to wander, and you find yourself missing the way that the world used to be. Like all those things that you used to do for fun."

"You used to do *this* for fun?" Riley mockingly shook the cords of her own nylon cage. "That says a lot about who you were before the shit hit the fan."

"Shit like this used to be part of my job," Everett combed the whiskers of his stubbled beard as he studied the spread of glass underneath the net. With a grunt of satisfaction, he turned back towards the house, but not before adding, "Special Forces. And if I'm being honest – trapping the enemy was always fun."

"Well, *I* meant the conveniences that we used to take for granted," Rose's chiding gaze followed her husband for a moment, before she took a seat underneath the shade of the tree. "You don't realize what you miss until it's already gone. We used to rely on electricity for so many things. Boiling the kettle. Using the microwave to heat up last night's leftovers.

Having a fridge to store those leftovers. Hot showers. Binging the latest TV shows. Those food delivery apps..."

"You could list a thousand things," Riley narrowed her eyes at the woman. "None of that shit has anything to do with why I'm strung up over your fucking driveway right now."

"I'm getting to that," Rose settled into her chair, taking a moment to appreciate their sunlit surroundings. "I remember that whenever it was nice out like this, I used to sit on the veranda. I'd sip a cold drink, listen to an audiobook, sometimes with a fan blowing a breeze beside me, and I'd just watch the day go by... You're here because I love your voice, Riley – and I'd like you to read for me."

Riley's head cocked slightly, unsure of whether she had heard the woman correctly.

Still frowning, her gaze flicked towards the sound of wind chimes ringing from the house again as Everett opened up the front door.

A freckled red-haired girl shuffled out onto the veranda.

The two captives locked eyes across the distance, their pupils dilating in recognition.

It was Heather's little sister – Taylor Seabrook.

CHAPTER 17

"You motherfucker!!" Taylor screamed at the sight of Riley.

She dropped what she was carrying, leapt down the veranda's stairs and ran towards the pinyon pine tree where Riley was suspended in the snare.

"Careful, sweetie, there's glass on the ground," Rose spoke over her shoulder as the freckled girl with braces drew close. "I'm guessing you two know each other?"

"Oh, you got that right, Mrs Lawson," Taylor spat from the edge of the gravel driveway, seething up at Riley. "This bitch broke into my house. She stole half our shit. And then my sister went missing. I haven't seen her since. She's probably dead by now. And it's all your fault, fucker."

Riley's heart sank for the girl.

She hadn't even stopped to think about how Taylor would react when they saw each other again.

Zack and Austin could have explained that Riley had only come to help, but there was no sign of either of them now.

And with Rose and Everett listening in, Riley couldn't even tell Taylor that her sister was still alive and in town, waiting for her – not without putting Heather and Dylan in danger.

"I told you not to come after us," was the only thing that Riley could think to say. Then, her brow creasing with clarity, she added, "Maybe if you'd listened, you wouldn't be in this mess right now. You'd still be back in Kansas with Heather, Austin, Zack, Demi and Dwayne."

She waited for Taylor to question how Riley could have known her friends' names.

But the girl's freckled face was still twisted with anger.

"What fucking mess am I in?" Taylor sneered, holding her arms out wide, mockingly glancing around at their sunlit surroundings. "I'm fed, I'm clean, and I haven't had to look over my shoulder in weeks. You're the one who's strung up like a fucking piñata out here. Oh, *please* tell me that's the only reason why she's still alive."

"No, and you know that's not how we do things," Rose pursed her lips with a mixture of patience and reassurance in her tone. "We invited Riley here to make your job a little bit easier, sweetie. So I expect the two of you to be nice to each other."

"And what if I don't cooperate?" Riley narrowed her eyes as Everett approached with the bundle that Taylor had dropped. "At this point, why should I have to listen to *anything* that comes outta your mouths?"

"That ditch outside is a real good reason," Everett shrugged indifferently, drumming his fingers against the stock of his assault rifle with a sinister smile.

"Do yourself a favor, Mr Lawson," Taylor began as she took a book and a paper fan from him. "Skip to the good part and nail this bitch in the face. And make sure you watch out for her two friends too. She's just the distraction. They're probably sneaking around back right now."

She's talking about Keith and Sterling, Riley knew.

71

But Keith Bowman was in Colorado the last time she had seen him, and Sterling Granger was probably down in Texas by now.

"I didn't see anybody else out there," Everett's penetrating gaze went from Taylor to Riley. His eyes lit up, and he immediately turned on his heel, striding back towards the house. "But she said *we* on the phone. Rose, watch these two. I'm getting the sniper rifle."

"That was Taylor-level dumb," Riley hissed through her teeth, clenching the cords of her nylon cage as she seethed at Heather's idiotic little sister.

Zack and Austin were still out there somewhere.

And Taylor had just lined up her own friends in the crosshairs.

"Where'd you hear that?" the freckled girl's voice cracked, her desire for vengeance giving over to spiteful curiosity. "*Taylor-level dumb* – who the fuck did you hear that from?"

"Girls," Rose interjected with a taut motherly tone, turning her head between them both. "It's a beautiful day, and I don't want my afternoon getting spoiled by the two of you bickering. Taylor, if you please."

Broken glass shards crunched underfoot as Taylor approached the snare, sullenly silent as she held up the book – a romance novel with a bare-chested man adorning the front.

Riley managed to clasp its covers with her gloved fingertips through the net's diamond-looped mesh, but the smutty book wasn't the only thing that passed between the two girls.

Searching each other's eyes, Riley knew that Taylor knew – Heather was still alive.

"I don't wanna keep her waiting too long," Riley said cryptically, feigning a glance at Rose. "Let's just do what we have to do, and we'll settle our shit later."

Taylor swallowed, before yielding with a meek nod.

"I'm glad you came around, sweetie," Rose sighed with a happy smile at the snare, completely unaware that Riley had been talking about Heather. "You had me a little worried there, because Everett has a nasty habit of getting rid of folks who don't seem worth the trouble. I'd hate to see that happen to you, too."

CHAPTER 18

"Maybe you'd feel more comfortable without those gloves on?" Rose Lawson suggested as Riley dropped the romance novel for the umpteenth time.

"No, it's not the gloves," she replied in a measured tone, guarded against giving up any more of her gear. "These are like a second skin to me now. I'm just not used to turning pages through a fucking fishing net."

"You won't be up there forever," Rose promised her, patiently waiting for Taylor to pick up the book again. "Why don't you take them off for a little while – just until we're done?"

Riley's gaze went from Rose to Taylor, who wordlessly urged her to follow the woman's instructions, glancing pointedly up at Everett posted on the ridgeline at the top of the hill.

The big brawny brute had been kneeling in his trench for hours, scanning their surroundings through the scope of his sniper rifle, warily watching for any signs of movement in the distance.

And occasionally, he would check back to make sure that Riley hadn't snapped any more cords of her nylon cage.

"Actually, could I get a glass of water?" Riley changed the

subject, massaging her throat. "It's heating up out here, and having to read to you this whole time sure hasn't helped."

"Just when the story was starting to get steamy again," Rose clucked her tongue in disappointment, before giving Taylor a resigned nod. "But – we do have to take care of that voice. Gosh, I miss being able to just play an audiobook."

"So, here's an idea," Riley began as they watched Taylor walk back towards the married couple's modest wooden house. "Why don't you just put up some solar panels on your roof? I mean, you managed to get that landline working just fine, what's a few more cables? And that way, you could charge up all those devices that you've been missing, plus you wouldn't have to worry about having to feed a couple of extra mouths. You could let us go."

"I said the exact same thing to Everett," Rose gave her half a smile at the suggestion. "I got outvoted on it though. The landline only needs a couple of batteries and a resistor. Low risk if anything goes wrong. Wiring up a bunch of solar panels though – that runs the risk of electrocution, or burning the house down, and it's not like we can hire an electrician nowadays. But even when we still had enough fuel to power our generator, I couldn't download any new audiobooks anyway. So, I'm sorry, sweetie, but you're just gonna have to stick around for a while."

She was outvoted on it, Riley had tuned out most of the woman's reply, but that part she had focused on. *That means there's more than just the two of them.*

Riley had figured as much from the strange tinkling noises coming from inside the house all afternoon, along with the plume of smoke rising from the chimney as the sun began its westward descent.

But she doubted the thought that either Rose or Everett would have given any of their prisoners the power to vote.

Otherwise the Lawsons would have already had solar panels.

The house's wind chimes rang again as Taylor emerged, still carrying Rose's book and paper fan, along with a glass of water.

Riley stifled the urge to gag as she eyed the book's cover again with disgust, dreading the thought of reading another word of the woman's smutty romance novel.

"I don't think I can hang around for much longer," her gaze met Taylor's, as if either of them had a choice. Riley glanced up at the orange tint in the clouds, searching for something that would convince the Lawsons to let her go. She took a gamble. "If I don't show up soon, my friends are gonna start looking for me."

"Well, good luck to your friends," Rose twisted her lips skeptically. "But I don't think you're ever gonna see them again."

"I told them I was coming here," Riley replied, struggling to wrap her gloved fingertips around the glass of water as Taylor handed it to her. "They don't mess around either. You're gonna have your hands full if the rest of my group has to come knocking."

"I'm sure we'll manage, sweetie," Rose smiled at her apparent concern. "My son and I held this place against dozens of raiders and looters – and that was long before Everett came home. I highly doubt that your friends are gonna fare much better, especially since they'll be going up against a Green Beret, too."

Riley began quenching her thirst, using the water to buy some time to think of something else to say, but by the end of the long swig, her mind was just as empty as the glass.

"Great," Rose took her seething silence as submission. She nodded towards the book in Taylor's other hand. "Shall we continue?"

Riley glowered down at the bare-chested man on the cover of the romance novel.

The idea of joining the ditch full of dead bodies was beginning to have its appeal.

"Come on," Taylor gazed up at her, eyes pleading with her to take the book. "It's not like you have to read it *and* fan Mrs Lawson at the same time." She glanced over her shoulder at Rose, quickly adding, "Which I didn't mind doing, by the way."

"Sweetie?" Rose tested impatiently, shifting in her seat.

Riley rubbed the back of her neck, feeling like a bird caught in a cage.

Her gaze searched the ground, before narrowing at Taylor's unbound hands and feet.

All Riley had to do was just keep on tweeting like a good little bird, and eventually, they'd let their guard down.

"Hey!" Everett suddenly yelled from the top of the hill, his keen stare turned towards the front of the property. "You see anything on your way back?"

Riley couldn't quite make out the reply in the distance.

"That must be Stan," Rose sighed, partially glad to hear that he was home, but with a look of longing at the book in Taylor's hand. She stretched in her seat before rising to her feet, meeting Riley's gaze, "My son. He's a nice young man. I think you two would get along well."

"Why's that, is he gonna let me go?" Riley snorted behind the mesh of the fishing net.

"Maybe," Rose tilted her head encouragingly. "But not until after we toss your friends into the ditch."

77

CHAPTER 19

"Taylor, sweetie, could you take my chair back to the house?" Rose Lawson asked, although it hadn't been intended as a question. She looked up at Riley, "Thank you for the wonderful afternoon. I have a feeling we're gonna be spending a lot of time sitting out on the veranda together."

"You're gonna need to let me outta this net before that can happen," Riley shot back, the slender muscles of her jaw flexing at the shameless woman.

"That all depends on how soon your friends come knocking," Rose shrugged as she turned her head to one side, smelling the scent of fried fish wafting over from the chimney. She savored the late afternoon air with a longing sigh. "I have to say, these past few weeks have been absolute bliss. Between having you for company, Taylor's help with the chores, and Demi's skills in the kitchen, you three girls sure are bringing back all those pieces of the old world that I've been missing."

What was the name of that kid's sister again? Riley furrowed her eyebrows, wondering what could have happened to the other missing girl. Her eyes lit up as she remembered, *Nancy.*

But before she could ask about her, Riley's ears picked up on something in the distance.

"Looks like we finally scored a hit in town," a young man's voice floated up from the other side of the hill. "Somebody triggered our spike trap in that alley behind the townhouses. They wouldn't have been able to walk away without help. I followed a trail of blood to a nearby backyard. Found two plates and a couple of critter bones. Must have moved off by the time I got there though."

"Probably those two who came looking for Taylor and Demi last time," Everett stood up to stretch as his son loped over the ridgeline.

In complete contrast to his father, Stan Lawson was a tall and lanky youth. His face was framed by twin curtains of shoulder-length brown hair, with a pair of glasses that flashed in the late afternoon sun.

"Right on time, Stan – smells like dinner's almost ready," Rose called as she pulled open the inner gate, the cowbell clanging its greeting overhead. "Everett, why don't you head on in? I'll take watch for a while. Bring me a plate when you're done eating."

The rugged soldier turned the thought over in his mind for a moment before nodding in deference.

Unslinging his sniper rifle, he gestured for his wife to join him on the hilltop, pointing out key positions for her to keep an eye on.

"Nice..." Stan slowed his strides as he approached Riley's snare, adjusting his glasses to drink in the sight of their new prisoner. He raked his gaze up and down the nylon cage, leering from Riley's grimy face down to her bare foot dangling from the bottom of the net, "... gloves. Those are some really nice gloves. Where'd you get them from?"

"Fuck off, creep," she scowled back at him, knowing full well that he didn't give a shit about where she had gotten her gloves.

"Sorry, I'm just really into survival gear," he mumbled, avoiding her glare as he sheepishly shuffled past, glass shards crunching underneath his boots. He called across to the veranda, "Hey, Taylor, heat up the water tank for me. I'm gonna take a bath after dinner."

This place is a fucking slave camp, Riley shook her head in disdain as the freckled girl obediently disappeared to carry out her master's bidding.

Riley remembered the rebellious redhead who she had met back in Kansas, wondering where all of the girl's aggression had gone now.

As far as she could tell, Taylor Seabrook had never been one to follow instructions.

The months that Taylor had spent separated from her big sister must have changed her.

Any number of things could have happened to the girl's group on their way over to Utah, but Riley held a sneaking suspicion that something bad had happened right here.

Because underneath all of the pleasantries and all of the *sweeties*, the Lawson Family was still savage enough to dispose of dozens of dead bodies in the ditch outside.

And judging by the way that they had put on a hell of an act just to lure Riley into a trap, she knew that these people were capable of doing anything.

Nancy's already dead, Riley had no doubt about that. *But maybe they forced Taylor and Demi to watch.*

The cowbell rang again as the big iron-barred gate swung shut behind Everett.

"This is military issue," he was holding Riley's confiscated combat knife in one hand as he approached, fixing her with his penetrating gaze. He cocked an eyebrow, "Did your father serve?"

Riley rubbed the back of her neck, staring down at the serrated edges of her own blade.

If she lied about her father, Everett would probably cut her some slack, being the purported daughter of a former brother-in-arms.

But then again, if he hit her with a follow-up question, she'd get caught out, and he'd just as likely gut her for the failed attempt at stolen valor.

Telling the truth about Nolan Armstrong's career as a police officer wouldn't work so well for her either though – no good father would let his daughter grow up without teaching her some form of self defense.

And with his level of training, she'd become an instant threat to the Lawsons.

As if she wasn't already.

"My dad was an accountant," Riley told him a much easier lie to maintain.

"Bullshit," Everett scoffed, instantly catching her out. "That's what I told my son to say about me whenever somebody asked. And you took way too long with that answer." He combed the whiskers of his stubbled beard for a moment, his eyes settling on her leg dangling from the hole in the bottom of the net. "Yeah, you definitely know more than what you're letting on. I think you might be more trouble than you're worth. And I don't wanna have to keep an eye on you all the time. Too bad for Rose, I suppose."

He advanced with the combat knife, his weathered face lined with rigid resolve.

Riley's eyes darted towards Rose posted on the hilltop.

But the woman couldn't help her now.

Or wouldn't – not against her own husband.

"That knife belonged to a man named Trask," Riley blurted out. Faced with certain death, she had to tell him the truth, or at least one version of it. "He was a soldier I met on the road. We got attacked back in Colorado and – he didn't make it. I was with him when he died. So if you're gonna kill me, at least don't use his knife to do it."

"Where was he stationed before The Fall?" Everett tested her, his murderous march stopping just short of the snare.

"Fort Rushcliffe," Riley replied on a shaky breath, glad that she could still recall the details of her group's conversation with Captain Drummond. "He went AWOL on the way over to Boston."

"Sounds like he made a good choice – at least until he met you," Everett grunted, eyeing her for an age in an instant before deciding to lower the knife. "Boston was a shit show."

"What the hell's happening over there?" she furrowed her eyebrows, flipping the focus back on him instead.

"Nothing good," the rugged soldier lifted his distant gaze to the spreading boughs of the pinyon pine tree, momentarily lost in its leaves. "I barely made it outta there alive."

"Did we get attacked?" Riley's curiosity got the better of her, despite still being caught in his trap and at his mercy.

The man was a Green Beret.

She couldn't even imagine what could have caused him to turn tail and run from a fight.

"Take a good look around – how else do you think it's gotten this bad?" Everett answered her with a question of his own. His stare hardened again, and his eyes traced over the snare before meeting her gaze. "Whole country's fucked now, same as you."

CHAPTER 20

Still suspended in the fishing net as dusk began to settle in, Riley Armstrong stretched her free leg down to the gravel driveway, trying to grip a shard of broken glass in between two of her toes.

At any time throughout the day, she could have pulled her leg back up through the hole in the snare, but she had been waiting for the cover of darkness before working on her escape plan.

She had no idea whether Zack and Austin were still hiding out somewhere in the woods, or if they had already run back into town to tell Heather what had happened. But if they were still hanging around, she figured that they would've been waiting for the night as well.

Slowly drawing her foot back inside the net, she took care not to slice her toes as she picked up the broken crystal with her gloved fingertips.

Riley's gaze went from Rose on the hilltop with the sniper rifle, to the Lawson Family's house, peering at the glowing windows as flickering firelight danced across the glass panes.

Keeping her movements small, she began cutting through the diamond-looped mesh. She made sure to only sever a few threads of each nylon cord, so that the net's overall shape still appeared intact at a glance.

Settling into a steady routine of fraying cords while avoiding the attention of her captors, Riley drifted back to the conversation that she'd had with Everett.

She had already decided that there was no reason for her to trust a single word that had come out of his mouth.

Granted, the country was still reeling from the asteroid and the failed missiles that had sprouted half a dozen mushroom clouds on the horizon – but that didn't mean that America had come under attack.

If anything, the government had probably decided to send all of their military forces to Boston – far away from the asteroid's falsely-projected impact site on the West Coast – and now they were just waiting for the lingering radiation clouds to dissipate, before sending in any organized recovery efforts.

Whatever was happening to the rest of the country wouldn't change her current situation though. She was going to live as a slave unless she tried to escape. She supposed that death could have been a third option, but death was never a choice – it was an absolute certainty.

A series of tinkling noises snapped her gaze back towards the house.

The moment her eyes traced over the windows, Stan threw open the front door and climbed down the veranda's stairs, with a chorus of wind chimes ringing in his wake.

Riley fumbled with the glass shard as he made a beeline for the snare.

"Hey, so I think we got off on the wrong foot," he stopped at the edge of the gravel driveway, trying his best to maintain eye contact this time, despite the gathering darkness. "I just wanted to ask if you were hungry. The leftovers are still warm, but I can tell Demi to re-fry the fish. It actually tastes better when it's been ref–"

"I don't want your fucking leftovers," Riley crossed her arms with a scowl, stealthily stowing the shard of glass behind the sleeve of her brown plaid shirt.

His face darkened as he pushed a curtain of his hair behind one ear.

"Fine, if you wanna be like that," he snapped hotly, looking back over his shoulder at the house before glancing up at his mother on the ridgeline. "I'm gonna have a lot of fun killing all of your friends when they come around. Maybe we won't let you down even after they're all dead. You can hang up here, hungry and exposed, until the smell starts putting us off our meals. Then we'll see how grateful you are for my fucking scraps. Get outta the way, you stupid bitch."

Stan lunged at the net, his long arms wrapping around Riley's trapped body to seize rough handfuls of her jeans through the mesh. Squeezing her thighs with a gag-inducing grin, he shoved her sideways, sending the whole snare swinging violently back and forth like a pendulum.

Heart in her throat, Riley's free hand shot up to grab a hunk of nylon at the top of the net, hissing and snarling as she struggled to keep herself from accidentally plunging a limb through the array of frayed cords.

The snare twisted and turned in her throes, her vision spinning and filling with blurs of blackberry bushes, moonlit ripples from the lake, the hilltop wreathed in darkness, and the hellish hues of dancing firelight emanating from the house's front windows.

And through it all, the cowbell clanged above the big iron-barred gate, with Stan loping up the gravel driveway towards the ridgeline, eagerly relieving his mother from sentry duty.

With the net rocking itself back into place again, Riley soon found the section of mesh that she had been wearing down, and she got straight back to work.

She had actually felt a measure of sympathy for the Lawsons – or for Rose, at least – right up until their cringey creep of a son had put his hands on her.

"You're gonna fucking pay for that," Riley promised under her breath, narrowing her eyes at his lanky silhouette in the distance. "Stupid bitch."

The cowbell rang again as Rose shut the gate behind her, and Riley stashed her makeshift wire cutter underneath her armpit once more.

"Is everything okay, sweetie?" Rose asked as she gave the snare a wide berth, trying to avoid treading on the broken glass crystals with her sneakers. "You must be hungry. Did you want me to boil you up some carrots and pass them through the net for you?"

"I'm fine, Rose, just leave me alone," she averted the woman's gaze.

As hungry as she was, Riley still had enough of her morals left intact to refuse a kindness from a mother who was about to mourn for her soon-to-be dead son.

"I know you wanna leave," Rose sighed knowingly, pursing her lips. "Believe me, I'd feel the exact same way if I was in your position. But you should ask yourself – where else do you need to be? Here, we can provide for you. I know it doesn't look like much, but we've got plenty of food, water and shelter for the six of us. You could make a life for yourself here. At least until all of this craziness in the world is over. I have no problem with letting you girls go, but not until after we know that it's

87

safe for you to go back out there again."

"Look, I appreciate you trying to be nice about this," Riley replied, just wanting the conversation to be over. "But if I'm being honest, right now, I'd feel a hell of a lot safer being out there than I do in here."

"Just give it some time, I'm sure you'll come around," Rose smiled up at her. "I'll see you in the morning, sweetie."

Riley's ears pricked up as the faint jingling of rocks against tin sounded from somewhere over the hill.

Zack and Austin are making a move, she realized, her pupils dilating as she remembered the rusty cans hanging all along the barbed wire fence.

She wished that Rose would just hurry herself back into the house already, but it seemed like the woman was waiting patiently for her to say *good night*.

Then, in the same instant that Riley's adrenaline had spiked, leaves began rustling overhead as a cool evening breeze blew through the boughs of the pinyon pine tree.

Fucking wind, Riley breathed out the tension in her muscles. *Fuck Zack and Austin, too.*

Rose was finally turning to leave, when she paused for a moment, frowning at the frayed fishing net in the dappled moonlight.

Riley's heart pounded in her ears as the woman drew closer to inspect the snare's mesh.

CHAPTER 21

Rose Lawson's sneakers crunched over the broken glass crystals as she narrowed her eyes at the frayed fishing net.

"Would you mind showing me your hands, sweetie?" she asked, her gaze laser-focused on Riley's glove underneath her armpit.

Beads of sweat erupted across the back of Riley's neck as she slowly held up her hands, gingerly clamping the glass shard against her ribs with her upper arm.

"Thank you," Rose tilted her head slightly, still studying the chafed snare, her lips pursed and unconvinced. "And now – just humor me here – lift up your arms for me."

Riley bit her bottom lip, unsure of how the woman would react to her escape attempt.

Rose was unarmed, but it would only take one shout to Stan on the hilltop for him to turn the sniper rifle on their new prisoner.

It wasn't like Riley had any other choice though.

She closed her eyes, drawing a shaky breath.

GUVV!!

The sniper rifle woofed a finger of hot lead, ripping through the night air.

Her heart froze in her chest.

Did that psycho just fucking shoot me!?

She couldn't feel anything.

It was as if her nervous system's pain receptors had been switched off.

The agony of a rifle round was beyond the range of what her body could register.

She dreaded the thought of bleeding out in the trap, unable to do a damn thing about it.

"CONTACT!!" Stan roared from the ridgeline, crouching in the trench as he lined up another shot at the front of the property.

Riley's eyelids snapped open again as Rose took off running up the gravel driveway back towards the house.

GUVV!!

Another lead hornet rocketed towards its target, followed by a garbled yell somewhere in the distance.

An icy spike of adrenaline surged through Riley's bloodstream as she realized – Zack and Austin had come through for her after all.

"Fuck, fuck, fuck," she muttered under her breath, her eyes tracing over the section of nylon cords that she had frayed so far.

It wasn't big enough to fit through yet.

She needed more time.

"Rose, get inside!!" Everett bellowed as he burst out of the house and leapt down the veranda's stairs.

The brawny Green Beret nearly bowled over his own wife in his haste.

He spun Riley around as he tore past the snare, ramming open the big iron-barred gate before he shot through and sprinted up the hill.

A dissonant chorus of wind chimes, cowbells and gunshots rang through the night, and in the cacophony of noise, Riley continued cutting open the fishing net.

She wasn't even worried about whether she'd be spotted now.

She wasn't going to get another chance like this.

"Read the fucking sign, assholes!" Stan shouted as he handed Everett the sniper rifle. "NO TRESPASSING!!"

"Shit," Riley cursed herself as the glass shard slipped from between her fingers.

She felt around the bottom of the net, hoping that the fragment's jagged edge had caught on something, but she had no hope of finding the shard in the darkness – not unless it sliced open her bare foot.

Fuck it – big enough, she decided quickly, grabbing handfuls of the frayed mesh and frantically ripping open a hole in the side of her nylon cage.

Riley managed to squeeze her head and one arm through, when the snare spilled over on its side, leaving her dangling halfway out of the tangled mess.

"Stan, head back, grab another rifle and climb up on the roof," Everett's rasping orders floated down from the hilltop in a lull of gunfire.

"But I wanna go after these guys with you!" Stan protested, even as he retreated from the ridgeline.

"I'll handle the ones out in the woods," Everett growled over his shoulder, ducking low as he disappeared over the hill. "But I need you to look after your mother in case there's any more."

Kicking and squirming her way out of the snare, Riley clumsily dropped down onto the gravel driveway, her gloved hands breaking the fall.

Pushing herself up onto her remaining boot, she hopped across the scattered broken glass, careful not to plant her bare foot on the ground until she reached the grass.

She threw her back against the trunk of the pinyon pine tree, just as the cowbell clanged above the big iron-barred gate.

Breathing heavily, Riley searched for something that she could use as a weapon, but all she could see in the dappled moonlight was a rope-bound boulder that had served as the snare's counterweight.

"Looks like you just got all your friends kil–" Stan cut his sneering gloat short as he realized that their new prisoner had already escaped. "How the fuck – oh shit, MOM!!"

His footfalls raced up the gravel driveway as he rushed headlong towards the house.

Heart hammering in anticipation, Riley waited until she could hear the patch of glass crystals crunching, before she ducked down and swept her leg out in a roundhouse kick.

She timed the trip perfectly, catching Stan's shin mid-step, sending him sprawling spread-eagled and face first into the gravel.

Groaning with his glasses knocked askew, Stan tried to push himself upright, when Riley caught him full in the face with the toe of her hiking boot, striking the side of his skull with the force of a footballer kicking a field goal.

"Who's the stupid bitch now?" she spat, glowering down at the crumpled heap of his stilled body.

A long shadow shifted across the yard as Rose's silhouette appeared in one of the front windows, peering out into the darkness.

CHAPTER 22

Riley Armstrong lay flat on her stomach in the grass, waiting for her would-be captor's silhouette to disappear before making her stealthy advance towards the house.

The shadow in the front window soon slid out of view, replaced by the hellish hues of flickering firelight emanating from within.

Like a prowling panther, Riley pawed her way through the grass towards the wooden veranda, listening for any sounds of movement.

But there was nothing.

Not even a creak.

The entire wooden house was holding its breath, waiting for her to make the next move.

Crawling out of the moonlight and into the darkness of the veranda, Riley soundlessly skulked up the stairs, her focus flitting from side to side between the two front windows.

A loose floorboard groaned as she stood upright again.

"Shit," she cursed under her breath, padding with her bare foot to one side of the front door, just in case Rose was holding a gun, ready to blow a hole through the wood.

With her back against the wall, Riley's gaze went to the moonlit hilltop in the distance, grappling with the idea of escaping with her life intact, leaving Taylor and Demi behind.

But she shook the thought out of her mind the moment it had appeared.

If she abandoned the two girls now, she would only be adding to the moral debt that she was already carrying.

And she was determined to make things right with the Seabrook sisters.

Flexing her gloved fingers, Riley gripped the door handle, turning it slowly.

But before she could ease her way in, the door burst open, light spilling outside, the overhead wind chimes clashing in chaos.

Riley instinctively jerked her hand back, narrowly avoiding the downward slash of a gleaming blade.

"What the hell did you do to my son!?" Rose yelled, thrusting a knife towards her navel.

A cold rush of adrenaline flooded Riley's bloodstream.

She slammed the palm of her hand into the woman's forearm, blocking the blow.

Grabbing her knife hand, Riley twisted her wrist, turning it almost a full rotation.

Rose yowled in agony, her shoulder rising involuntarily as she lurched outside.

"Less than what he deserves," Riley snarled through gritted teeth, locking the woman's arm behind her back. "Drop it."

She glanced down at the serrated edges of the combat knife – Rose had tried to stab Riley with her own blade.

Taking advantage of the momentary lapse in concentration, the seemingly sidelined woman spun on her heel, driving her other elbow into Riley's temple.

"Fuck," she stumbled back a step, fumbling her grip on Rose's wrist as her vision blurred.

Powering through the daze though, Riley dropped her shoulder and rammed into Rose from behind, shoving her head-first into the door jamb.

Taking no chances, Riley seized two handfuls of the woman's hair and threw all of her own bodyweight inside the house, wrenching Rose around and sending her careening over the coffee table.

With some distance in between them now, Riley quickly sized up her surroundings, blinking blearily in her punch-drunk stupor.

The whole room was cluttered with furniture.

The dining table and kitchen stood on one side of the entrance, with the living area on the other, along with a doorway in the corner leading to a narrow corridor.

Recovering quickly, Rose leapt to her feet by the roaring fireplace. Framed by the infernal flames as she growled in anger, she swept her hair up out of her face and kicked the coffee table to one side.

Shaking the clouds out of her vision, Riley adopted a fighter's stance, turning at the torso with her palms raised like a pair of coiled vipers.

Rose gave her a thin smirk as she mimicked her posture, left foot forward and right foot back, the combat knife a serrated extension of her fist.

Should've known, Riley narrowed her eyes at the woman. *Of course a Green Beret's wife would know how to hold her own in a fight.*

She waited for Rose to advance on the attack, before twisting around, grabbing a wooden dining chair and swinging it like a gigantic baseball bat into the woman's side.

But Rose caught one of the chair legs with her free hand, and instead of retreating, she pulled herself closer to Riley, slashing and stabbing with the blade, aiming for her neck and arms.

Riley's pupils dilated as she evaded the thirsty edge of the combat knife, dodging each thrust and alternating her grip on the seat.

Snarling in exertion, she went back on the offensive, using the chair to steer the woman sideways, throwing her off balance before driving her backwards.

"You could've had a good life here," Rose spat as her sneakers squeaked and stumbled across the floorboards. "Now all you'll get is a bad death."

"Speak for yourself, you slave-driving bitch," Riley growled, forcing the woman up against the fireplace, stomping on her knees and kicking her feet backwards into the open flames.

Rose yelped as the scorching blaze licked at the backs of her legs, hacking wildly with the knife until the fire was too hot to handle. Overwhelmed by the pain, she threw the blade across the room, using both hands to wrestle for control of the dining chair instead.

Riley's head whipped around to see where the combat knife had fallen, determined to end the fight as quickly as possible.

Rose seized advantage of her distraction.

Spinning the seat out of Riley's grip, the woman tossed the chair aside and delivered a savage palm strike to her solar plexus.

Robbed of breath and staggering backwards, Riley fought to wheeze the air back into her lungs, resisting the urge to double over so that she could keep her eyes trained on Rose.

"Taylor, Demi," she huffed in desperation, her voice barely audible above a whisper as she glanced at the doorway in the corner leading to the narrow corridor.

"That's gonna leave a scar," Rose hissed sharply as she studied the singed backs of her legs. "I'm gonna set your fucking face on fire for that, you ungrateful little bitch."

Riley stumbled backwards into the sharp corner of the wooden kitchen island, but with her winded diaphragm, she couldn't even utter a gasp at the pain.

Still backpedaling, she dragged out dining chairs in her wake, buying herself a few more precious moments to recover as her eyes desperately darted and crawled across the floor for the fallen combat knife.

Rose skirted around the kitchen island, not even bothering to undo the pitiful attempt at a blockade.

And that's when Riley saw it – a knife block standing in the back corner of the kitchen.

Both women locked eyes for an instant, before lunging towards the set of blades.

Despite having no breath left in her lungs, Riley was quicker on her feet.

She had one hand outstretched, when a dishcloth smacked her in the side of the face.

Riley's hands blindly scrabbled and searched across the countertop as she tried to shake off the wet rag.

Suddenly though, her vision cleared again, and her gloved fingertips fumbled with the end of a knife's handle, before she was wrenched backwards by the neck.

"Didn't you hear me?" Rose breathed in her ear, tightening the dishcloth around Riley's throat, throttling her from behind. "I'm not stabbing you to death. I'm *burning* you to death. The last thing you'll ever know is the smell of your own skin melting off your skull."

Riley's vision swam as blood rushed to her head.

Already starved of oxygen, she was too weak to claw the choking cloth from her neck.

Throwing her leaden elbows back at the savage woman's ribs would have little effect.

And stomping her one hiking boot wasn't an option either – if she could manage to actually hit something – she could barely even stand up straight.

"You can struggle and scream all you want," Rose menaced, pulling the wet rag even tighter around her windpipe, "Because I want those two girls to hear *everything*."

With her eyeballs on the verge of exploding, Riley was out of options.

Then, in one final act of sheer desperation, she raised one heavy arm into the air, reaching back until she caught hold of a handful of Rose's hair.

Riley let her knees buckle, dropping all of her bodyweight.

Rose shrieked in agony as both women lurched forward.

Hip slamming into the edge of the kitchen counter, Riley's free hand shot out, and she ripped a chef knife from the block.

Savagely thrusting behind her, she plunged the blade deep into Rose's thigh, carving through flesh as she yanked it upwards, until the dishcloth dropped from around her throat.

Riley sucked in shallow lungfuls of air, painful but sweet, before pulling the chef knife free from the woman's thigh and spinning around on her heel.

Rose staggered backwards into the wooden kitchen island, staring down in numb shock as her own blood spurted and pulsed from the slash in her leg.

"That's gonna leave a scar, sweetie," Riley whispered hoarsely as she stumbled towards her would-be captor.

Blood sprayed her face as she sank the knife into the side of Rose Lawson's neck, the two women staring into each other's eyes as Riley opened her throat from ear to ear.

CHAPTER 23

"Fucking took you long enough," was the first thing that Taylor Seabrook could think to say the moment Riley unbolted their bedroom door.

"I'd lock you back in here if it wasn't for Heather," Riley croaked as her gaze locked onto her missing hiking boot stashed in one corner of the room.

"Where is she?" Taylor's eyes widened as she remembered the possibility of her older sister still being alive. The freckled red-haired girl stuck her head out into the narrow corridor before whirling back around, "Why isn't she with you?"

"I'll take you to her," Riley brushed off the girl's questions, keeping the information to herself as she sat down to pull on her sweat-stained sock and boot. She was being cautious, on the off-chance that Taylor would be stupid enough to leave her behind if she knew where to find Heather. "We need to get outta here – fast."

"That's gonna be a problem," Demi swayed on her feet with an odd tinkling noise.

Riley furrowed her eyebrows at the pale brunette looking pointedly down at one of her shoes.

A jumble of pet collar bells had been attached to her laces like a set of crude tracking devices.

"Are you serious?" Riley frowned at the two girls before drawing her combat knife from the strap on her thigh. "Why the hell didn't you take these off the second you heard those gunshots out there?"

"We didn't think you'd actually pull through for us," Taylor crossed her arms defensively, before exchanging a sidelong glance with her friend. "We didn't wanna risk trying to escape again unless we knew for sure."

"It's not the bells that are the problem," Demi brushed away a tear as she watched Riley slicing through the pet collars. Her voice cracked with a strained sob as she explained, "After we tried to escape the first time, they cut off my toes as punishment."

Riley's raw throat stung as she swallowed grimly.

Any remaining ounce of misguided sympathy that she had felt for the Lawson Family instantly disappeared.

"Come on," she tossed the severed pet collars aside and rose to her feet, supporting Demi as they stumbled out into the living area. She glanced over her shoulder on their way over to the front door, "Taylor, grab some knives from the kitchen."

"Damn – you really have been rolling with Heather," Taylor raised her eyebrows as she stopped beside the wooden kitchen island, admiring Riley's handiwork. Her smile turned into a scowl as she glared down at Rose's bloody body, before aiming a set of angry kicks at the corpse of their former captor. "Read your own fucking books. Fan your own fucking face. Wash your own fucking dishes, you two-faced slave-driving piece of shit!"

"You already killed them all, right?" Demi asked as Taylor's screams of rage died down.

"I still need to finish off Stan," Riley's pulse quickened as she considered the chance that he might have already woken up. "Then we need to hit the road before Everett comes back."

She left Demi to disable the wind chimes above the door before going over to the window, cupping her hands over her peripheral vision as she peered out into the night.

Riley's breath fogged the glass as she let out a sigh of relief at the sight of Stan's motionless figure, still lying face down in the gravel driveway.

"I want the chef knife," Demi laid claim to her weapon of choice as the three young women left the house and made their way down the veranda's stairs. She narrowed her eyes at Stan on the ground, "I hated that fucking creep from the day we got here. Let me handle him."

"No, you're too slow," Riley quickened her pace, leaving the other two behind. "You girls go on ahead and get up that hill. I'll be right behind you."

"Stan was the one who cut off Demi's toes," Taylor explained as they trailed along in Riley's wake. "Besides, Everett might hear that cowbell above the gate when we leave. I'm gonna need your help taking it down."

Riley's gaze flitted between the two girls.

Despite her desire to end Stan for putting his hands on her while she had been caught in the snare, she knew that it was nothing compared to what he had done to Demi, and whatever else he had subjected both girls to during the past few weeks of their grueling captivity.

"Make it quick then," Riley finally nodded, not wanting to deny Demi the catharsis of revenge. She glanced at Taylor before turning towards the moonlit hilltop, "Why should we go out through the front though? We should go around back and find a way through those blackberry bushes. We might get a few scratches, but it's better than taking a chance on running into Everett out front."

Demi scoffed at the idea as she gladly limped towards Stan, each one of her lopsided steps filled with fervor, while the bloody chef knife shone with a sinister gleam in the moonlight.

"That's how we got caught last time," Taylor spoke over her shoulder as she made a beeline for the big iron-barred gate. "It wasn't just the brambles that we got tangled up on. These sick fucks decided to put concertina wire in between the bushes too. Now shut up and give me a boost."

Riley's tongue pressed against the inside of her cheek as she snorted at the girl's idea of gratitude for helping them escape, but she leaned back against the gate all the same, clasping her gloved hands together against her thigh.

Just as Taylor hopped up, a high-pitched yelp of startled agony filled the night.

Peering past Taylor's hip, Riley could see Demi's arm working furiously in the dappled moonlight underneath the pinyon pine tree, her savage thrusts continuing long after Stan's screams had fallen silent.

"So much for this making all the fucking noise," Taylor jumped down with the cowbell, pinching the clapper in between her fingers.

She stashed the primitive alarm in the thick brambles of a nearby blackberry bush, while Riley ran back to Demi, helping the hobbling girl out through the gate and up the hill.

"I can't see Everett anywhere," Taylor whispered from the trench as they caught up to her on the ridgeline. "I think we're good to go."

"He might be watching from the woods after all that noise,"

Riley shot an accusing sidelong glance at Demi.

"Well, I'm not waiting around to find out," Taylor decided abruptly, standing up and starting down the hill, "Because I do *not* wanna be here when he gets back."

Riley bit her bottom lip, pausing for a few moments before following the impetuous girl, but not without glancing back at the house one last time.

It felt as though she had forgotten something.

"Hey, check this out," Demi fished something out from her pocket when they were halfway down the hill, proudly holding up a bloody souvenir. "For all those times he said I smelled *amazing*. Ugh."

"Nice one, why didn't I think of that?" Taylor gazed sidelong at the severed nose in Demi's hand with a rueful grin. "I should've cut that bitch's ears off while I had the chance."

"Tell me you finished him off though," Riley shrugged Demi's arm from around her shoulder, passing the pale brunette over to Taylor.

"No, I just knocked him out again," she replied casually, dropping Stan's nose onto the gravel driveway and grinding it underneath her heel, before kicking the squashed fragment of flesh into the sea of overgrown grass. "When he wakes up, he'll know what it feels like to lose something he can never grow back."

"You fucking idiot," Riley stopped in her tracks, shaking her head in disdain as she turned to climb back up to the ridgeline. "Did you even think about what's gonna happen when those two start coming after us? And here I thought Taylor was the dumb one."

"Who the hell are you calling dumb?" the rebellious redhead bristled beside Demi. "You're the one who hasn't thought it through. That creep can't put his glasses back on without his nose, so he'll barely be able to see shit anyway. And when Everett gets back, he's gonna have to spend all his time looking after his son instead of coming after us. If you kill Stan now, we'll have a fucking Green Beret on our asses no matter how far we run."

"I just killed his wife," Riley reminded them both as she started back up the hill. "Everett's coming after us no matter what. And I like our chances a hell of a lot better if there's only one of them."

Just as she finished her sentence, a twig snapped in the woods on the other side of the highway.

CHAPTER 24

Riley instinctively dove for cover in the field of overgrown grass lining the gravel driveway, with Taylor and Demi plunging in after her.

The tall stalks of grass towered overhead as they crawled in deeper, straining their ears for any more sounds coming from the forest on the other side of the highway.

The moon hung high in the starry sky for what felt like an eternity, the night filled with crickets chirping, foxes laughing, and the forlorn hoot of an owl.

"It was probably just a fucking animal," Taylor whispered impatiently, pushing herself up.

"Stay down!" Riley hissed, her gloved hand shooting out to pin the girl to the ground.

"Hey, what the f–"

Riley shushed her as the owl's hoot came again, closer this time.

She knew that she was probably just overreacting, but she preferred to look like an idiot rather than risk getting killed because of an idiot.

Demi was shaking beside Taylor, staring wide-eyed into the

wall of grass, probably reliving the trauma of her maimed foot as the thought of being recaptured pervaded her mind.

Guess I'm the idiot this time, Riley finally supposed with a heavy sigh, hearing nothing beyond the evening's wildlife.

She was about to take her hand off the back of Taylor's neck, when the unmistakable sound of boots scuffing the asphalt reached their ears.

Riley locked eyes with her, the freckled girl swallowing her spite as the front gate's latch *clacked* open.

The entrance's hinges squeaked in the heart-hammering stillness before the gate swung shut again, setting off a chain reaction of rattles from the rusty tin cans hanging all along the property's barbed wire fence.

Staring into Taylor's eyes, Riley could remember the same look of fear frozen on Hayden Marsh's face, unable to do anything but watch as a muscle-bound mountain lion stalked from the shadows towards its petrified prey.

A rash of gooseflesh flowered down her arms as they listened to Everett's footsteps crunching up the gravel driveway behind them, uncertain of whether they had crawled far enough into the field of grass, but unwilling to risk even a muscle twitch to make sure – just in case the movement would give away their position.

Then, the footsteps stopped.

He couldn't have been more than a few yards behind them.

Despite the icy flood of adrenaline rushing throughout her entire body, Riley remained completely still, not even daring to breathe.

Taylor was limp on the ground with her eyes shut, as if playing dead would save her from the hulking brute.

Silent tears streamed down Demi's face as she continued

staring into the wall of grass.

Buck up, princess, Riley's gaze flicked between the pair of girls. *We're all in the shit now.*

Immobile as she was, her mind was racing, rehearsing the motions of springing up, drawing the combat knife strapped to her thigh, and lunging for Everett's throat, all in one fluid motion.

She visualized his death over and over again – but it would only take one slip-up, one fumble, one misstep, and the muzzle of his sniper rifle would be the last thing she'd ever see.

The owl's forlorn hoot sounded again, but this time, it came from Everett's lips.

Pulse pounding in her ears, it took all of Riley's willpower not to reach for her knife.

Seconds stretched for an eternity in the stillness before Everett took off running.

"ROSE!?" he roared, his footfalls disappearing over the ridgeline. "STAN!!"

Riley gave herself permission to breathe again as she nodded at the other two, preparing to push herself up, when she felt a dull prick against the palm of her gloved hand.

She furrowed her eyebrows at the spiky clump of weeds, before catching a metallic glint in the moonlight.

It wasn't a clump of weeds at all.

It was a cluster of nails that had been embedded into the rubber tube of a garden hose.

Demi stifled a groan as she tried to rear up on her knees, the spike-studded rubber tendril pulling taut as it rose up with her, another chunk of shrapnel half-buried into the side of her stomach.

"Don't you fucking scream," Taylor urged as she clapped a

hand over the pale brunette's mouth.

Riley gripped the garden hose on either side of the cluster of nails, waiting for Demi's reluctant nod before ripping the barbs out of her torso.

Despite Taylor's gag and the determination lining Demi's face, a squeal of pain escaped from the maimed girl's lips.

But the sound was nothing compared to Everett's thunderous bellows of grief and anguish rising up into the night, the recently-widowed Green Beret cursing their names as he swore brutal and bloody vengeance on the three escapees.

CHAPTER 25

"Move your fucking legs, bitch," Riley grunted as she supported Demi in between her and Taylor, the three young women crashing through the forest's undergrowth together.

"We should've taken the highway," Taylor snarled through clenched teeth as she almost tripped over a rock.

"And risk getting caught out in the open?" Riley snorted as she glanced over Demi's arm draped around her shoulder, searching for a viable path through the trees. "No, we need some cover if we're gonna make it back into town alive. We'll link up with the rest of your group and work out a way to deal with these assholes from there."

A gigantic felled tree blocked their path – the wall of decomposing wood too high for Demi to climb, and too close to the roadside to skirt around the base of the trunk – forcing the trio deeper into the forest.

"Do you think I'm gonna get tetanus now?" Demi fretted over her weeping wound in a slight daze as they followed a game trail down into a broad moonlit gully. "What a shitty way to die."

"You'll be fine," Riley set her mind at ease, wanting the girl focused on putting one foot in front of the other. She scanned the silvery terrain for an easy slope up out of the gully so that they could get back on track. "Trust me – I almost sliced my fingers off on a roof gutter back in autumn, and I'm still here. Plus, Heather's sitting on a bunch of medical supplies right now. We'll take a proper look at your stomach when we get back. Taylor, make sure you keep that pressure up until we get there."

"Yeah, I got it," she huffed, craning her neck as they stumbled past a dead rabbit hanging in midair, the dangling critter caught in a snare. "What if we have to split up later though? You haven't even told us where we're going yet."

"There's a reason for that," Riley replied in a taut tone, trying to keep her frustration to herself as the gully's slope became increasingly impassable with every step forward. "We're getting back to Heather together, or not at all... Ah, fucking finally."

Riley let out a sigh of relief as they reached the end of the gully, shuffling around the corner of a sheer moss-grown rock face. She could breathe a little bit easier now that they were at least traveling parallel to the highway again.

They followed a stony path in between the wall of rock on their right and a sharp drop on their left, their steady breathing in the night's stillness interrupted only by the sounds of a stream burbling away somewhere in the distance.

Riley shrugged Demi's arm from around her shoulder as the path narrowed, leaving the two girls to walk side by side. She didn't want to risk losing Heather's little sister over the side of the cliff, especially not after all of the trouble that she had gone through just to get her back.

"Alright, this looks like a good spot," Riley stopped to size up a grassy slope at the end of the rock face. She glanced back over her shoulder at the other two, "We should be able to get back up to the highway from here."

"You guys probably could," Demi balked at the steep angle, the incline offering nothing to hold on to. Her eyes turned downcast, gazing from her bleeding torso to her maimed foot before shaking her head knowingly, "I'm not gonna make that."

"What if we just keep going this way?" Taylor glanced pointedly at the path curving around to the left. She shrugged at Riley, "You're the one who said we need to stay outta the open anyway."

"Alright, fuck it, let's go," Riley took the lead, not wanting to waste any more time trying to convince them otherwise.

With Everett and Stan hungry for revenge, she knew that every second would make a difference.

The path widened as it began to slope downwards, and Riley threw Demi's other arm over her shoulder again as she peered into the moonlit foliage below.

The forest's vegetation had grown a lot thicker at the bottom of the slope, and the trees were standing closer together, but at least the landscape had leveled out. There even seemed to be a much more manageable incline on the far side of the patch of undergrowth – one that they could use to work their way back up to the road.

Stumbling through the wild weeds and ferns infesting the flat forest floor, Riley steered the two girls through a natural corridor in between the trees.

They were making their way around a particularly large leafy shrub, when Riley's boot stepped on something dense that gave way underneath her heel.

Whipping up out of the vegetation with a whistle, a long

wooden stake smacked her square in the face, sending her reeling backwards.

The three escapees fell to the forest floor together, but Riley's elbow somehow went *through* the ground. She flailed out with her other arm, grabbing a handful of Demi's shirt before she could fall any deeper into the hidden rift.

"What the fuck, Riley!?" Taylor seethed as she clambered to her feet.

"Oh, no..." Demi stared horror-struck past Riley's shoulder, tears welling in her eyes. "No, no, no, no, no!!"

A hollow wooden *thud* sounded as Riley pulled herself up out of whatever hole she had fallen into, rolling back onto solid ground beside Demi.

She furrowed her eyebrows as she drew herself up on her hands and knees, searching for the void that had almost swallowed her whole.

"Can somebody tell me what the hell's going on?" Taylor's spiteful curiosity went from Demi's strained sobs to Riley's confused pawing at the forest floor.

The strange square of ground gave way again, and a camouflaged trapdoor swung open to reveal a shadowy pit, filled with the metal teeth of garden stakes half-buried in the dirt, their sharp ends pointing upwards.

And impaled at the bottom of the spike pit, with his curly blonde hair strewn across the lower half of his face frozen in agony, Austin stared lifelessly up at the moonlight filtering down through the foliage.

"Shit," Riley swallowed at the sight of his glassy eyes, his hands wrapped around the bloody garden stake protruding from his chest.

Taylor and Demi's eyes filled with the sight of their dead

friend, lips trembling as they gawked open-mouthed at his corpse, even after the trapdoor swung shut again.

Still on her hands and knees, Riley peered into the vegetation at her feet, only to see the plastic prongs of a garden rake that had knocked her off balance.

"They knew we'd come this way," she realized, retracing their trail through the forest. Just like the alley behind the row of townhouses, the Lawson Family had used the environment to their advantage, funneling their prey into a trap. She rose to her feet, seizing Demi and pulling her upright, "Come on, we've gotta keep moving." She clicked her fingers at Taylor, trying to snap some sense back into her, "Hey, we need to stick together. Just don't let go of Demi. These traps weren't made for three."

She had no idea whether that was true or not.

Maybe they had just gotten lucky.

Maybe there was another trap capable of taking out all three of them at once.

But there was one thing that she knew for sure – if she hadn't been holding on to Demi, she would have joined Austin at the bottom of that pit.

Riley took a moment to size up their surroundings, glancing back over her shoulder at the natural corridor in between the trees leading up towards the highway.

She had no doubt in her mind that there would be even more traps hidden in the dense shrubs, just waiting to be triggered.

Over the sounds of the two girls sniffling in grief, she could hear the stream again, its waters burbling somewhere nearby.

At least we wouldn't be stomping through the underbrush anymore, Riley supposed, trying to pinpoint the stream's location.

"What do we do, Riley?" Taylor's voice cracked as her teary

eyes scoured the forest floor, utterly unable to discern which way would lead them to safety – not when only a few careless steps could mean certain death.

"We go back," Riley decided grimly, retracing their path as best as she could remember.

Holding on to each other tightly, the three young women shuffled their way through the thick patch of shrubs, each of them sharing the unspoken knowledge that they might not get so lucky when they came across the next trap.

And with the two remaining Lawsons capable of predicting their escaping prisoners' movement patterns, it felt like they would never find their way out of these woods alive.

CHAPTER 26

"We're almost there, look," Taylor took her hand off Demi's wound to point between the trees, silvery slivers of the stream's waters rippling in the moonlight.

"Slow down for a second," Riley cautioned, holding the two girls steady as her sharp eyes traced over the muddy banks lining the creek. "Let's not take any chances."

Demi's knees gladly buckled as Taylor eased her down gently, the pale brunette gingerly prodding at the glistening red patch staining the side of her torso.

"Don't get too comfortable," Riley reminded them both as she scanned every dimly-lit inch of their shortest path towards the stream.

"I just need a minute," Demi replied before exhaling slowly, her gaze focused on the ground as she silently summoned the strength to keep going.

"How deep do you think the water is?" Taylor wondered as she peered through the foliage at the silvery stream again. "Maybe we could let Demi float on her back while we pull her along."

"There," Riley ignored the question as she pointed out a nylon cord tied between two trees, partially hidden by tufts of grass growing above the stream's bank.

She ventured closer to get a better look, her gaze following another cord from the midpoint of the tripwire back to a tangle of underbrush piled at the base of a weeping willow tree.

Crouching beside the pile, she gently blew away the dry leaves and detritus, revealing a tethered stick behind the trap's trigger mechanism – a pair of hooked branches barely holding on to each other – with one thick branch half-buried in the dirt, while the other was suspended in the air by another length of taut cord, the tough nylon rope leading up into the cascading leaves of the willow tree.

And lurking above it all like a gigantic spider poised to pounce on its prey, a huge log hung overhead, ready to swing down on a pair of ropes bound to another sturdy bough looming above the stream's muddy bank.

Riley rubbed the back of her neck as she studied the lethal trap – the swinging log was easily the width of her rib cage, and long enough to catch all three of them from behind, knocking them all face down into the water, either with their skulls cracked or their spines snapped.

"You've gotta be fucking kidding me," Taylor groaned as she stopped beside Riley, her eyes fixated on the monstrous log menacing above their heads. "How the hell are we gonna outrun these guys when they already know where we're gonna be?"

"We can't," Riley finally allowed herself to admit the horrible truth aloud. Still stooping beside the trap's trigger mechanism, her eyes went from Taylor to Demi, "This is their home. Their forest. Their town. We're not outrunning them."

"Don't tell me you're just gonna give up," Demi grunted as

117

she pushed herself to her feet, wincing in pain as she staggered over to join them.

"No, but we need to change our mindset," Riley replied as she cautiously extracted the tethered stick from behind the trap's trigger mechanism before tossing it into the stream, rendering the tripwire useless. She rose to her feet again, "We've been running scared this whole time. That's exactly what's gonna get us killed. That way of thinking – that weak and helpless mentality – that's how they've been able to predict our next moves."

"What else are we gonna do – stay here and fight them instead?" Taylor scowled skeptically before throwing her arm around Demi, steering the wounded girl towards the stream. "Good luck, bitch. We're gonna go with Plan A. Thanks for volunteering to buy us some time though."

"Go ahead then, I'm not stopping you," Riley fired back with a hard stare.

She had already done more than enough to help them both escape.

When she could have easily saved herself, she had decided to turn back, kill Rose, and free the two girls from their slave-like captivity.

But if they were just going to leave her to deal with the Lawson Family's forthcoming vengeance alone, then Riley could – at the very least – consider herself cleared of her own moral debt to the Seabrook sisters.

"You're not coming?" Taylor faltered above the stream's muddy bank as she glanced back over her shoulder, second-guessing her own resolve at Riley's indifference.

"I'm not playing into their next trap – no," Riley decided as she looked up at the huge log suspended in the air again. "You two wanna run off like scared little girls? Then see how far you get, because that's exactly who they're looking for. You're only gonna get yourselves killed – and Heather too, if you can even make it back into town alive."

"Come on, let's go," Demi urged Taylor, holding her wounded torso as she climbed down the muddy slope without a backwards glance.

"Just wait a second," Taylor held up a hand, turning to face Riley as Demi waded into the shallows behind her. "Where's my sister? You still haven't told us how to find her."

"I wasn't exactly paying attention to the street names," Riley admitted truthfully as she stood beside the weeping willow tree.

She knew that she would have to rely solely on the town's landmarks – if and when she wanted to find her way back to Heather and Dylan.

But what would she tell them?

I found your sister, Riley played out the conversation in her head. *And then I let her get herself killed.*

Taylor's eyes softened as she silently pleaded with Riley for Heather's whereabouts, the impetuous girl standing in the direct path of the swinging log, completely oblivious that the trap could still be triggered without the tripwire.

"We're wasting time," Demi called over her shoulder, moments before slipping on a rock and falling in the stream. She hissed through clenched teeth as she clambered upright again, "Just leave her here if she wants to stay."

Riley's gaze flicked between the two girls.

She knew that they wouldn't last the night by themselves.

She flexed her gloved fingers before locking eyes with Taylor.

"Stick with me, and I'll take you to Heather," Riley promised, her eyebrows raised in earnest.

"Fine," Taylor bristled, as if the word had left a bitter taste on her tongue. She looked over her shoulder, "Demi, come back."

"No chance," the soaked brunette scoffed as she stumbled downstream. "I'm putting as much distance between me and those psychos as possible. If you come back to your senses, I'll meet you at Josh's house – but I won't be staying there for long."

"You better have a good plan," Taylor seethed as she turned back to face Riley again.

"Trust me," Riley leaned against the willow tree's trunk, clasping her gloved hands together against her thigh with half a smirk. "These guys don't know who they're fucking with."

CHAPTER 27

"How long are we just gonna sit up here for?" Taylor asked for the umpteenth time, her voice hushed against the sounds of frogs croaking and raccoons chittering in the moonlit hours of the early morning.

"As long as it takes," Riley whispered back in a waking doze, having almost nodded off.

She rubbed her eyes for a moment and shook herself back into vigilance again, before staring down at the ground, sternly reminding herself of how high up they were.

From their perch in the upper boughs of the weeping willow tree, the swinging log trap's trigger mechanism was barely visible through the cascading leaves – but it also gave Riley the confidence that she and Taylor were equally as hidden from view.

Within arm's reach was the taut nylon rope anchoring the huge log in place, winding over a thick branch and stretching down to the base of the trap's trigger.

Riley's plan was simple – wait for Everett to investigate Demi's footprints along the stream's muddy bank, and then cut the cord, using the man's own trap against him.

"What if he's not even coming?" Taylor voiced her growing doubts as they listened to the nocturnal animal noises rising above the stream's incessant burbling. "Maybe this whole time – he's been burying Rose and fixing up Stan's face after what Demi did to him. What if he's decided to wait until dawn before he comes after us? And we're just wasting our time up here while we could be getting away."

"Oh, he's coming," Riley knew. She gazed intently between the branches at her obscured view of the silvery stream. "Do you really think a man like that is just gonna wait around before he goes after the people who killed his wife?"

"But how would he even know which way – "

"Shut up for a second," Riley shushed, her arms budding with gooseflesh as she sensed a shift in the air.

Leaves rustled without the wind as the surrounding wildlife silently retreated.

It was as if the forest had suddenly become aware of the pair of trespassers in its midst, the towering trees conspiring to absorb all of the ambient noises of the night, engulfing the two escapees in an eerie stillness.

Even the burbling waters of the silvery stream seemed to lull to a whisper, while rippling moonlit glints winked up at Riley and Taylor, pinpointing their perched positions within the weeping willow's leaves.

Breathing shallow, Riley's sharp gaze flicked towards a flash of movement in the woods on the other side of the stream.

Twigs snapped as a branch bent backwards, disappearing into the dense darkness of the thick forest, and in its place emerged a sinister specter – a malevolent spirit of the woods – the stealthy silhouette manifesting itself into the shape of a man as it silently stepped out into the moonlight.

The bloodthirsty shadow of Everett Lawson materialized, garbed and painted in mottled shades of forest green, completely camouflaged from head to toe. Only the whites of the widower's wild eyes remained, but even those had changed.

In the wake of his wife's death, the rugged soldier's savagery was no longer simmering just beneath the surface of his weathered face.

Now, the yearning to succumb to his primal instincts was on full display, the big brawny bear of a man armed to the teeth and ravenous for revenge.

"You see something?" a barely audible whisper emanated from the darkness of the trees behind him.

Fuck, Riley flexed the slender muscles of her jaw, silently fuming as she slowly drew the combat knife from the strap on her thigh. *He's not alone.*

She had expected Everett to be hunting them down by himself, especially given Stan's mutilation.

Her plan was still sound, but catching them both at the same time was going to be a challenge.

"Footprints," Everett growled as he sloshed his way across the stream, zeroing in on Demi's tracks along the muddy bank. His gaze snapped towards the tripwire's tethered stick bobbing up and down on the water's surface nearby, "One of them came through here and disabled the trap."

"Only one set of prints?" Stan came out from the shadows, breathing heavily through his mouth. A thick bandage was wrapped around his face, with a ruddy maroon stain flowering where his nose had once been. "Sounds like whoever's left had to learn the hard way to watch where they're walking."

He shook with spiteful laughter, but only a short-lived bout of stifled panting escaped from his lips as he joined his father in the shallows.

Adjusting the sniper rifle's strap around his shoulder, Stan studied Demi's footprints before gazing downstream, the side of his face giving off a dull sheen in the moonlight. Underneath his curtain of hair, a strip of duct tape was holding his glasses in place.

Riley clenched the hilt of her combat knife, taking care not to make any sudden movements that could give away their position.

Taylor sat perfectly still on a nearby bough, her petrified gaze constantly crossing the distance in between the blade's serrated edge and the swinging log's suspension cord.

Pulse pounding in her ears, Riley watched as the vengeful father and son duo stood in the shallows beside the muddy bank.

Despite the adrenaline coursing through her veins, she held her combat knife steady, just inches away from the nylon rope, unable to spring the trap just yet.

Without having seen the swinging log in action, there was no way for her to accurately guess the trajectory that it would follow, and the height that it would hit.

If she cut the cord too early, she could risk missing the two men completely, the huge log swinging down only to sail right above their heads.

As much as she hated the anticipation, she had to wait for the right moment to strike.

She only had one shot at catching them both by surprise.

"You go on ahead," Everett finally rumbled, his penetrating stare tracing a path from Demi's footprints to the trap's trigger mechanism. "I'll find the other two."

Riley's heart leapt up into her throat as his glare lingered on the willow tree's trunk.

She was sure that with one long look at the upper branches of the tree, the merciless Green Beret would soon recognize their silhouettes hiding within the leaves.

Biting her bottom lip, she brushed her blade against the load-bearing cord, bracing for the worst.

But to her relief, Everett's attention dropped down to his tactical vest.

"Here, take these," he turned to Stan, handing him what appeared to be a pair of metallic pinecones. "Remember, one — and I'll come running. Two — and I'll kill anything that moves. So when you see me coming, you know the signal."

Riley's dilated pupils locked eyes with Taylor for an instant as they both realized what was being exchanged.

"I won't need them," Stan boasted, even as he secured the pair of grenades within the pockets of his hunting vest. "These bitches don't deserve quick deaths."

"Do whatever you have to do," Everett growled as he climbed up the muddy slope and stepped over the defunct tripwire. "But if you're gonna take your time with them, start with the legs and work your way up. Just don't take any chances with Riley. Kill her on sight."

With a reluctant nod, Stan turned to head downstream.

Swallowing at the sight of the two men splitting up, Riley tightened her grip on the combat knife, still holding the taut nylon rope in between the blade's serrated teeth.

Everett was definitely walking through the kill zone now, with his eyes trained on the shadowy ground as he tried to pick up the trail.

Riley would have preferred to hit both of their pursuers in one fell swoop, but with Stan already heading downstream, she could at least catch Everett off guard.

After all, out of the two remaining Lawsons, the brutish Green Beret posed the biggest threat.

With one slash of her knife, the log would hit him with enough force to either crush or cripple him.

It was now or never.

CHAPTER 28

"Some fucking plan that was," Taylor finally broke her seething silence as soon as they were at a safe distance upstream.

"I couldn't risk cutting the cord, and you know it," Riley shook her head as they waded through the shallows. She had been expecting this argument from the moment that she had allowed Everett to safely pass underneath the weeping willow. "Stan would've turned around and spotted us in the tree, and we'd both be dead or dying before we even hit the ground."

"But there's two of us and only one of him," the hot-headed girl strained to keep her voice low as she argued. "Do you really think that that lanky creep could've figured out what was happening, shouldered his rifle, and fired off two rounds with *any* accuracy before one of us knifed him in the fucking face?"

Riley was about to point out that their knives would have been no match for a sniper rifle, until she remembered that she'd been similarly armed back in Colorado, when her group had been tasked with clearing out the purported cannibals from Leadthorne High.

"We had them, and you let them go," Taylor scowled sullenly

as they approached another bend in the winding stream. She glanced back over her shoulder, "Now Demi's the one who's outnumbered."

"Yeah, well, maybe Demi should've finished off Stan when she had the chance," Riley countered unapologetically as she craned her neck to peer around an upcoming bend in the stream. "Then things would've gone exactly the way I'd planned it, because Everett would've been the only one left for us to worry about."

"We can still go back," Taylor switched her tone from accusation to appeal. "Maybe if we're quick enough, we can catch up to Stan and hit him from behind. Then we'll take his gun, throw one of his grenades, and wait for Everett to show up."

"Bad idea," Riley flexed her gloved fingers, just in case she'd have to catch Taylor by the arm and drag her along. "If Stan's ducked back into the trees, he'll see us go straight past. Even worse, we'll be making a whole lot of noise just trying to catch up to him."

"So, what – we're just gonna leave Demi to fend for herself?" Taylor huffed, frowning sidelong at her.

"She had a good head start," was the only consolation that Riley could offer. She glanced up at the navy blue tint staining the darkness of the early morning sky. "Come on, it'll be daylight soon. It won't take long before Everett works out that we're still alive. He'll follow our trail straight back to the stream."

Dreading the thought of the vengeful Green Beret hard on their heels, Taylor's shoes churned through the shallows as she picked up the pace.

The current grew stronger around their feet as they approached a ford strewn with debris – but on closer inspection, they realized that the stream had been cluttered with detritus by design.

Narrow channels had been dug out of the ford, providing evenly-spaced intervals of clear waterways through the crossing. Gill nets and funnel traps had been strategically placed at the ends of each bottleneck, using the artificial currents to drive any passing fish into the snares.

Even now, Riley could see their glistening scales shimmering underneath the water's surface, the fish either too tangled or too weak to escape and swim back upstream.

Light from the edge of dawn filtered down through the forest's foliage, and Riley spotted something on the dimly-lit ground as she picked a path in between the fishing traps.

Furrowing her eyebrows, her pupils dilated as she recognized two sets of footprints crossing the ford.

"This is their trail," Riley realized, her gaze following the heel tracks to a well-worn path leading back into the forest. She turned towards Taylor, "That's where they came from. If we cut through here, I have a feeling it'll take us straight back to the highway."

"But what if they've set up more traps along the way?" Taylor balked at the shadows in between the trees, her feet frozen in place.

"It's possible," Riley acknowledged, rubbing the back of her neck as she climbed out of the shallows. "But we're gonna run into another trap sooner or later. Everett's got this whole forest rigged. Who knows – maybe he's even got bear traps on the other side of this ford to keep the local wildlife from getting at the fish. We're just gonna have to take a chance and hope that he hasn't set up any more traps along his own trail."

"Well, hold on," Taylor frowned as she pondered aloud. She

jerked a thumb over her shoulder, "The town's that way. If we were running scared, that's the way we'd go. That's the way Demi went. But you said that's how they've been able to predict our next moves." She turned the thought over in her mind before nodding in agreement, "They probably weren't expecting anybody to come this far upstream though. Yeah, this is our exit. It's gotta be."

"Glad you were listening," Riley gave her half a smirk before offering a hand to pull her up onto the ford. "Maybe you're not as dumb as Heather says after all."

"Yeah, you got that right – after you," Taylor smiled sarcastically as she gestured for Riley to take the lead. "So after we get back into town and meet up with Demi, we're going straight to my sister, right?"

"Only after I'm sure we're not being followed," Riley paused to pick up a fallen branch, tapping at the ground as they started on the trail. "Until then, we've just gotta keep doing whatever they aren't expecting us to do."

They climbed up a steep incline along the dirt path, with the trees thinning out on one side, until they were walking along the edge of a cliff overlooking a valley.

Riley took her eyes off the trail for a moment just as the full vibrancy of dawn broke out across the sky, shedding light on the deadly path that they had taken on their escape.

Splayed out below was the thick vegetation infesting the flat forest floor bordered by the snaking stream. There was the narrow stony path that wrapped around the sheer moss-grown rock face. And finally, the broad gully beside the gigantic felled tree that had funneled them down into the Lawson Family's lethal series of traps in the first place.

And along the edge of the cliff was the perfect position

for somebody with a sniper rifle to look out over the valley, watching as each of their victims died one by one, without even having to squeeze off a shot.

Riley's shoulders shivered involuntarily as she thought of the fish that had swum through the waterways of the ford, only to be caught in a snare, frantically flailing in futility as they awaited their deaths.

But at least she and Taylor had been smart enough to figure their way out.

The path took a turn away from the sniper's perch, heading back into the trees.

Riley probed at the ground with her branch, making sure that there were no more hidden tripwires or trapdoors, when a piece of wood whistled through the air, striking her square in the face.

CHAPTER 29

A distant scream roused Riley Armstrong from her apparent slumber, her eyelids fluttering open.

She was lying on her side, with her cheek on the dirt path, dust motes swirling with every ragged breath as she blinked blearily at a nearby nest of gnarled tree roots.

Distorted voices floated down from above, sounding both near and far, but their words were incomprehensible in her groggy daze.

How the fuck did they get around us?

Riley's heart sank as she remembered that this was the Lawson Family's territory.

Their home.

Their forest.

Their town.

And she was just the escaping prisoner who had killed their wife and mother.

A man's shadow loomed over her, either Everett or Stan, eager to take his revenge.

Riley flexed the slender muscles of her jaw.

Well, you're gonna have to fucking earn it.

Icy adrenaline flooded her veins, and her hand flew to the combat knife strapped to her thigh.

But her gloved fingertips only fumbled and scrabbled at an empty sheath.

Forced to fight without a weapon, she powered through her punch-drunk stupor, rolling sideways towards the network of gnarled tree roots and springing upright.

But before she could get her bearings, the dizzy spell threw her off balance, sending her stumbling backwards into the twisted trunk of a juniper tree.

"Hey, calm down, it's me," a warped voice cut through the haze of confusion as a familiar face approached warily. "Sorry about the hit. Looks like I got you good – I wasn't expecting you guys to show up along here."

Zack's messy brown hair blew in the early morning breeze as he ventured closer, picking a cautious path in between the juniper's tree roots. He held out one hand towards her, with his other arm clinging to his chest, bandaged and swaddled in a sling.

"Fuck – I thought..." Riley frowned at the coppery taste of blood in her mouth as she searched left and right for Everett and Stan. Her voice was deep and unnatural in her own ears, "What the hell happened to you? And where's my knife?"

"I'll explain in a minute," he swallowed as his outstretched arm lingered in the air. His voice dropped a hint of urgency as he added, "First things first though."

She was about to knock his hand aside, preferring to regain her balance on her own, when Zack's eyes betrayed a crucial detail that she had missed.

Glancing sideways, Riley's heart leapt up into her throat.

She was standing along the edge of the cliff, with only the

juniper's twisted tree trunk to stop her from plummeting down to a grisly death.

Her hand shot out, latching on to his forearm as she whole-heartedly accepted his assistance, pulling herself back over to the dirt path again.

Swaying on her feet, Riley let out a shaky breath before gently cradling her temples, waiting for her daze to dissipate.

Down in the valley below, birds trilled their morning songs as they flocked from one thicket of trees to another, like a group of ants crawling across the forest's green canopy.

A few yards down the trail, Taylor stood alone, silently staring off into the distance.

Another far-off scream reached their ears.

"Just end it already, you piece of shit," Taylor clenched her fists in rage. She bristled at the sight of Riley standing in her peripheral vision, "That cringey son of a bitch caught up to Demi."

"He's fucking *torturing* her," Zack's eyes turned downcast, unable to ignore the screams of the maimed girl's prolonged suffering.

"There's nothing we can do now, she'll be dead before we get there," Riley stated the obvious, just in case either of them were feeling brave – or stupid. Sidling closer, she took Taylor by the arm, gently easing her back up the dirt path towards the trees again. "Come on, we've gotta get outta the open."

"First we hear Dwayne's dead, now it's Austin – and Demi's next," Zack choked on his own words as he stooped to sling his backpack over his good arm's shoulder. "I fucking hate this town."

"Wait – Dwayne's gone too?" Taylor shrugged out of Riley's grip, glaring sidelong at her, as if his death had somehow been her fault. "Why didn't you tell me?"

"What difference would it have made?" Riley's face hardened as she gave them both the cold truth, "Mourning your dead friends isn't gonna get us outta this shit any faster."

"Fuck you," Taylor mumbled, averting her sullen gaze as she stubbornly followed them along the trail.

Riley supposed that if the roles had been reversed, she probably would have said the exact same thing to Taylor.

But they didn't have the time or the luxury to shed any tears.

They had to stay focused if they wanted to stay alive.

"Hey," Riley's gaze settled on Zack as he took the lead, "The knife, remember?"

"Yeah, right here," he croaked, fishing into his backpack's side pocket and handing the blade back to her. He cleared his throat before adding, "I figured I'd hold on to it until I was sure you weren't gonna use it on me again. Once was enough for me."

"I guess we can call it even now," Riley's forehead throbbed where the piece of wood had struck her. She cocked her head slightly as she slipped her combat knife back into its sheath. "So, how'd you end up along here?"

"We waited all day yesterday for you to come back out onto the highway," Zack glanced back over his shoulder, not even bothering to check the path ahead for traps. "We figured something bad happened to you, so we started looking for anything we could use to our advantage, and that's when we found this trail. The plan was to wait until they changed guards again before we ran across the highway. Then we'd cut through the barbed wire fence, sneak in, break you out, escape through the woods, and then eventually circle back into town."

"Did you even make it through the fence?" Riley remembered

the faint jingling of rocks against tin just before Stan had started firing his sniper rifle. "I could hear you guys coming – did you forget about all those rusty cans hanging around the perimeter?"

"No, we got them," Zack shook his head with a sigh. "Grass was tall enough to hide behind after we got to the ditch. We cut down the closest cans, set them aside, crawled underneath the fence... and then Austin kicked the whole pile of cans over. By accident, probably, but he panicked when the bullets started flying. He even ran the wrong way. I got hit in the shoulder when I tried to go after him."

"And now he's dead," Taylor mumbled in a forlorn voice behind them. "You never should've split up. *We* never should've split up."

Adding a bleak weight to her words, Demi's scream of agony rose up in the distance again, long and loud, followed by a gunshot.

Finally, Riley blinked somberly as the forest absorbed the lingering echoes.

"Fuck these guys," Zack was the first to break the silence. "I saw them coming through here, but I had to hide while I was patching myself up." He wiped his face before looking back over his shoulder at Taylor, "But don't you blame me for what happened to Austin. I didn't think he'd die just because we split up. I thought eventually, he'd –"

"No, I mean *us*," Taylor cut him off, her breath hitching in strained sobs. "I mean *me*. Back in Kansas. I shouldn't have run off. All I wanted to do was get our shit back. I didn't think that the tour bus would catch Heather and Dwayne. I didn't think that the rest of us would have to walk all the way to Utah in the middle of winter. I didn't think that I'd get three of our friends killed. And for what? All because I wanted to waste this bitch and take back everything she stole? She doesn't even have her fucking backpack anymore."

"Hold on," Riley stopped suddenly in her tracks.

"Oh, fuck off," Taylor shoved her from behind, but feebly. "Whatever you're gonna say, I don't wanna hear it. Just take me to my sister."

Riley could have apologized to her, for stealing their supplies and setting their group down this dark path of death and despair in the first place.

She also could have argued that both her mother and Abbie Granger were pregnant at the time, and that most of the stolen food had been put towards making sure that they were still eating enough to support their growing babies.

Or she could have reminded them that she had traveled all this way, rescued Taylor from a family of sadistic slavers and wrought the wrath of a Green Beret, just so that she could reunite the Seabrook sisters and make up for what she had done.

But just like mourning their dead friends, none of those conversations would have any impact on whether they would survive the relentless pursuit of Everett Lawson and his son.

"You mentioned my backpack," Riley began, her brow creasing with clarity. "Zack, how fast do you think you can run with that shoulder?"

CHAPTER 30

"I never wanted to see that house again," Taylor huffed as they crested the hill, her feet suddenly growing leaden at the sight of their former prison. "I still can't believe we're coming back here."

"Exactly – this is the last place that they'll be looking for us," Riley replied between ragged breaths as their shoes tore up the gravel driveway.

The big iron-barred gate stood wide open, and the ruined snare trap still hung from the lone pinyon pine tree. It seemed that in the wake of Rose's death, the remaining members of the Lawson Family had abandoned any desire to protect their home.

"So, what's the plan here, Riley?" Zack panted as he glanced around the property, only just now seeing it for the first time. "Are we digging in and defending, or are we laying a trap of our own?"

"That depends on what we can find inside," she called over her shoulder as she bounded up the veranda's stairs, a loose floorboard groaning underneath her boot. "We need to be fast though. If there's nothing that we can use, and they catch us here, we're never gonna leave this place alive."

Riley pushed open the front door, sweeping her gaze from the living area to the kitchen.

The early morning sunlight streaming in through the front windows cast shadows over the remnants of her violent clash with Rose, most of the big room's furniture either pulled out of place or upended.

The dining table was strewn with the hastily-scattered contents of a first aid kit, along with discarded wads of gauze, thick and crusty with Stan's dried blood.

The fireplace still had the dying embers of last night's flames, giving a sinister sheen to the trail of ruddy brown patches staining the floorboards, leading from behind the wooden kitchen island, and around towards the narrow corridor where the bedrooms were.

"Zack, you keep watch," Riley jerked her head over towards one of the windows as she and Taylor followed the trail of blood.

The door to the master bedroom creaked open with a mournful whine, and shadows danced across the walls as a candle's flickering flame burned low on the nightstand.

Rose Lawson's body lay in the center of the bed, with a sheet of linen draped over her bloody corpse. An impression in the blanket marked the spot where Everett had sat grieving beside his dead wife.

"Fucker," Taylor bristled as she pushed past Riley, the impetuous girl going straight for the nightstand as she looked down with contempt at the dead woman's body. "Don't forget – this bitch made Demi cook them dinner the same day that Stan cut off her toes. You thought her screams out there in the forest were bad? I can still hear the way she was crying while she was stumping around in the kitchen... They made me watch."

139

Without an ounce of remorse for the Lawson woman, Riley's sharp eyes scoured the room, flitting from the closet, to the bathroom door, to the dresser, before settling on the dark outline of her backpack lying in the corner.

She knelt down beside her pack, rifling through its contents while Taylor pulled out the nightstand's drawers and shook them out over the floorboards.

"It's not here," Riley drew a breath of encouragement as she shouldered her backpack. "He must've put it with the rest of his stash."

They were looking for her pistol.

Even though Riley had run out of bullets, the Lawson Family seemed to be well-stocked.

If there were any firearms and ammunition left in the entire town, this was the best place to find it.

Riley crossed the bedroom over to the closet and threw the doors out wide, searching high and low before tearing out shoe boxes and suitcases and stacks of clothes, scanning each of the shelves in the dim candlelight.

Taylor cursed under her breath as she worked over the dresser, scattering socks and belts and old documents across the floor.

A pair of footsteps scuffed the floorboards out in the corridor, and both scavengers whipped their heads around to see Zack standing in the doorway.

"Shit," Riley's eyes were wide with alarm, her hand dropping to the hilt of her combat knife. "Don't tell me they're already back."

"They're not – I just figured this'd be faster with the three of us looking," Zack answered as he stepped into the room. He shrugged, "Besides, if they come back and we still haven't found anything, we're dead whether we see them coming or not."

With that, he began stomping his sneakers around different sections of the floorboards, listening for any differences in sound.

"This is starting to get ridiculous now," Taylor huffed as she tore the dresser's bottom drawer off the rails and checked the space underneath. Clambering to her feet with an exasperated sigh, she tried her luck inside the bathroom instead. "They've got a big-ass sniper rifle out there, where the hell do they put it when they're not using it?"

Riley finished patting down the clothes hanging in the closet, having hoped to at least find some spare rounds hidden – or forgotten – inside a pocket of one of the jackets.

She stooped to try the discarded pair of suitcases again, picking up each one with ease and giving them both a shake, listening for a rattle.

But there was nothing.

"Hey, give me a hand with this," Zack called over his shoulder as he bent over the bed, hooking his good arm underneath the mattress.

Giving Rose's shroud one final remorseless glance, Riley leaned over beside him, curling her gloved fingertips in between the bed and its base.

Without missing a beat, they flipped over the mattress, sending the dead woman's stiff corpse crashing to the floor. The candle on the nightstand leapt with the impact, while hanging picture frames rattled against the walls.

"Where the fuck else would it be?" Zack scratched his head before prodding around the bed base's blank canvas. "Don't tell me we're gonna have to check the rest of the house."

"I *really* don't wanna go through that creep's bedroom,"

Taylor replied as she emerged from the bathroom, her search proving equally as fruitless. But with a reluctant sigh, she went over to the doorway anyway, her eyes on Stan's room across the hall, "I bet he's got something in there though."

"Hold on," Riley cocked her head slightly, peering at a picture frame that had been knocked askew across the room. "You guys see that?"

She picked up the candlestick from the nightstand and skirted around the overturned mattress, holding the flickering flame closer to the wall.

A horizontal crack had appeared in the wooden paneling, one that normally would have been obscured from view behind the picture.

Riley flipped the hanging frame off its hook, revealing a small niche hidden within the wall, housing a metal handle and a combination lock.

"Jackpot," Zack traced his finger over the crack in the wall, following a disguised outline all the way down to the floor. "This is a door. I'll bet these guys have a fucking armory back here."

Riley fought to contain her excitement.

There was a bounty of weapons on the other side of the wall.

They would finally be able to fight back against Everett and Stan on a level playing field.

"Okay, but how are we getting in?" she frowned up at the combination lock.

"That's the easy part," Zack shot her a wink as he turned towards the corridor. "Well, at least compared to finding the damn thing. We're gonna need some tools for it though. Somebody watch the driveway, I'll check the garage."

"Don't bother," Taylor lingered beside the hole in the wall, crestfallen. "The garage is locked too – side door and the roller."

"So, we'll find something else to crack it open," Riley pushed past Zack and started towards the kitchen, hoping to improvise with some cooking utensils instead. "What do you need?"

"A pair of bolt cutters would be nice," he quipped, clucking his tongue in the corridor. "Fuck it, let's try this other room."

Zack took half a step towards Stan's bedroom, throwing open the door.

He snorted in surprise, and a slow smile spread across his lips.

CHAPTER 31

Standing behind Zack, Riley craned her neck to peer through the doorway of Stan Lawson's bedroom.

Pin-up posters of bikini models plastered the wooden wall above his tightly-tucked bed. An assortment of canned foods had been neatly stacked on his desk in the corner. And two rows of small taxidermy animals had been arranged on top of his dresser, their lifeless eyes staring at the crack of sunlight shining in through the room's closed curtains.

But on the floor beside the dresser was a green and white toolbox, with its carry handle flipped up and ready for action.

"Now we're in business," Zack grinned, his eyes trained on the toolbox.

"Wait!" Riley hissed, elbowing him in the shoulder – the wounded one – before he could set foot in the room.

"What the fuck, Riley!?" Zack snarled in pain as he cradled his arm in the sling, gingerly prodding at his bandage. "What the hell are you thi–"

"Look," she pointed at the bottom of the doorway. "Watch your step."

A small length of fishing cord had been drawn taut half a

foot above the floorboards, barely visible in the dimly-lit room, but betrayed by a thin layer of dust that had settled across the string.

"Had my eyes on the prize," he admitted sheepishly, still wincing from the pain in his shoulder. He studied the room from the safety of the corridor again. "As much as I fucking hate these guys, I've gotta admit – they know what they're doing. All those posters on the wall, all that food on the desk... the floor's the last place you'd even think to look."

"Don't go in there," Taylor warned as she stepped out from the master bedroom, shuffling into the hall behind them to peer at the toolbox on the floor. "We can't use that. We can't use anything in here. We need to leave – right now."

"What are you talking about?" Riley furrowed her eyebrows, staring at her sidelong.

"Yeah, I'm not giving up now," Zack agreed as he took an exaggerated step over the tripwire. "These bastards are gonna pay for what they did to Austin and Demi."

Just as he finished his sentence, a loose floorboard groaned underneath his sneaker.

CRACK!

Red fragments sprayed up from the toes of his shoe as lead pellets hit the ceiling.

"FUCK!!" he bellowed in agony.

Zack flailed out with both arms as he stumbled forward.

He caught himself on one doorjamb.

But his busted wing fell short of the other.

Riley's pupils dilated as he spun through the doorway.

Her hands shot out, clawing for the back of his shirt.

But it was too late.

He had already blundered through the tripwire.

145

A gray streak flashed downwards from above the door frame.

And a sickening *squelch* sounded just as Riley caught a grip of his shirt.

Zack swayed on his feet as his entire body went limp, suspended by a pair of blades skewering the side of his neck.

The huge spiked mace – an abomination of wood, concrete and knives – shook as Zack's hand fell from the doorjamb, his head slumping forward, gurgling out his death rattle.

Riley stood frozen behind him, still holding the back of his shirt in gaping disbelief.

"I told you," Taylor's breath hitched in strained sobs. She balled her fists, pounding both Riley and Zack in a blind teary-eyed rage, "I fucking told you we had to leave!"

"But there's a toolbox right there," Riley murmured as she staggered backwards, only managing to block half of the blows, but too numb with the shock of their grievous oversight to feel the other half. She stared at Zack's body hanging in the doorway as she turned her mind back to the plan, trying to justify his sudden death so that it wouldn't be in vain, "We get the tools. We crack open the armory. We get the guns. And then we wait."

"Oh, you're gonna get the tools?" Taylor backed off, switching over to a verbal attack instead as angry tears tracked down her face. She jabbed a finger past Zack's dangling body into Stan's bedroom. "Go ahead – get the tools, Riley. But I bet you won't now, since everybody's so intent on doing the *exact – fucking – opposite* of whatever I say. I'll tell you what's inside that box. It's Stan's fucking fishing gear. Zack just got himself killed over some fucking tackle!!"

Taylor-level dumb, Heather's words rang hollow in Riley's ears.

She turned her back on the grisly scene, leaving Taylor alone in the corridor as she detachedly walked over to one of the couches in the living area, sinking into its soft embrace.

Riley had barely even known Austin, Demi and Zack – at least outside of what Heather had already told her about them.

And she had lost plenty of people who she had been much closer with – members of her own family included.

But at a time when it was impossible to know who to trust, each of their deaths made a massive impact on their chances of survival.

Out of the Seabrook sisters' entire group, Taylor was the only one left standing now.

All of their friends were dead.

Heather could barely walk with her wounded leg.

And there was no way that Riley was going to ask Dylan – a kid who looked barely in his teens – to help them kill a merciless Green Beret and his sadistic son.

You're the only one who can bring her back safe, Riley shook her head with a small snort as Heather's voice entered her thoughts again.

At this point, it seemed that Taylor was doing a much better job at keeping herself safe.

But that didn't mean that Riley was wholly incapable.

"Alright, I'm done with all this running around bullshit," Taylor croaked as she stepped into the living area, bitterly wiping away the last of her tears. "Can we just go back to my sister already before I push you into the next tripwire – uh, what the hell are you doing?"

Riley looked down at the combat knife clenched in her hand.

While she had been lost in a world of her own thoughts, she had been slashing long cuts into the couch's upholstery, gouging out clumps of foam from the cushions.

Taylor shifted her weight, edgily glancing over at the front door.

Riley exhaled a long breath as she sheathed her blade.

"If we can't use their own weapons against them," she began as she rose to her feet. "Then I'm gonna make sure that they can't come back here and use them against us either."

With that, she scooped up the pile of foam and tossed it into the fireplace.

"Won't they see the smoke from the forest though?" Taylor frowned as the flames from the fire's embers instantly leapt up to devour the foam. "They'll come straight back here – and we've got nothing but knives to fight them off with."

"Yeah, they will come straight back here," Riley echoed as she picked up a dining chair next, turning it sideways and pushing its legs into the fire's hot coals. "That's exactly what I'm counting on."

CHAPTER 32

"They'll see that burning from a mile away," Taylor glanced back over her shoulder at the black plume of smoke rising up into the clear morning sky. "But what if the fire gets outta control?"

"Then we're fucked," Riley wasn't going to pull any punches as they ran back into town, remembering how her Grandma Eleanor had single-handedly started a wildfire that swept across half of Nebraska. "But at least they'd be dead too."

Their footfalls echoed along the deserted suburban street, with abandoned cars and houses flashing past on either side as they worked their way towards an avenue in the distance.

"So, why don't we just go straight back to Heather and get outta town?" Taylor puffed, frowning sidelong at her, as if the answer was that simple. "We could use the fire as a distraction and get a head start – while we still can."

"We wouldn't get that far with Heather's leg," Riley panted, grimly remembering how Demi's head start had worked out for her. "No, running isn't an option."

"Then we should've used their own ditch to ambush them," Taylor belatedly realized as they passed by a storm drain clogged with windswept debris. "You know – pretend we're just two more dead bodies that they left to rot on the side of the highway. Then when they came home to put out the fire, we could've jumped up and knifed them in the back."

"That's if they didn't notice two new dead bodies lying right outside their gate," Riley shut down the idea – as if turning back around was even an option at this point. "Besides, I'd rather have us holding the home-turf advantage."

"Alright, we're nearly there," Taylor slowed down as they approached a semicircular score of corpses scattered around the next intersection. "But how do you know that they're even gonna come out this way?"

"Trust me – I know," Riley's dogged jog became a wary walk as she caught her breath. "After they're done watching their house burn down, they're gonna come looking for us at your cousin's place next. I can guarantee that Demi told Stan where we were supposed to meet up, just so that he'd stop and put a bullet into her."

An uneasy silence fell between them as they rounded the corner of the small strip mall, taking a wide berth around the delivery truck that had been rammed halfway inside the gun store on the end.

Lengths of barbed wire glinted in the sun, catching Riley's attention as they passed by the blockades and barricades strewn haphazardly across the parking lot.

She paused in the middle of the avenue, cocking her head slightly at the strip mall.

"What the hell, Riley?" Taylor panted a few yards up ahead, staring back at her. "We shouldn't be stopping until we get to Josh's house."

"I have an idea," Riley replied cryptically, before picking a path through the concrete no-man's-land. "Watch out for any tripwires."

"We already searched this place," Taylor huffed in annoyance, but she followed her lead across the parking lot all the same. "You saw how thorough we can be, so believe me when I tell you – there's nothing here."

"Nothing you were looking for," Riley agreed as she stopped in front of a toy store. "Did you check in here?"

"Yes," Taylor rolled her eyes, before sweeping a hand at every store in the strip mall. "Every single one's been cleaned out. Shelves, front counter displays, vending machines and staff lockers. Stock rooms, break rooms, back offices and maintenance closets. All empty. Whatever you're hoping to find, it's not here."

"I have a feeling it might be," Riley replied with half a smirk, pushing open the toy store's entrance.

A small bell chimed an apprehensive welcome above the door, and her boots crunched across shards of glass as she stepped over a broken gumball machine lying on its side.

Taylor begrudgingly followed her inside, arms crossed with a skeptical scowl.

"We're gonna need more than just knives to take these guys out," Riley spoke over her shoulder, thumbing the straps of her backpack as she scanned the aisles. Finding the section that she had been looking for, she smiled back at Taylor, "It's time we got a little firepower on our side."

"You're not making any sense," the impetuous girl stared up at the shadowy toy boxes lining the dusty shelves. "There aren't any paintball guns in here. What are you gonna do – kill them with foam darts?"

Riley peered at the names and descriptions on each cardboard box, before picking out one model in particular – an air-pressurized water gun, complete with a hand pump and reservoir.

"What's the one thing that you can always find, but never need?" she asked Taylor with a sidelong glance.

"Idiots who get everybody else killed," Taylor fumed, pointedly glaring back at her. "There's no shortage of that."

Riley's smile faded, holding the girl's gaze for a long moment before shrugging off the implication.

Both of them knew that the only death that she had been directly responsible for – at least in this town – was Rose Lawson's.

Everybody else had made their own decision.

"Try again," Riley broke the brief silence as she whipped out her combat knife, cutting the water gun free from its shell. She even gave the girl a hint, "Your cousin had them at his house."

"Fucking – furniture?" Taylor's scowl deepened with frustration. She glanced back over her shoulder at the avenue, "Who gives a shit? We don't have time for this. They could've given up on putting out the fire already. For all we know, they're heading over to Josh's place right now."

"Cleaning chemicals," Riley answered her own question. She cut free another water gun as she continued, "Bleach, disinfectant, laundry detergent, furniture polish, stain remover, dishwashing liquid... if you get a chemical burn in your eyes – in any fight – it's game over."

Taylor's face lit up in sudden realization, before nodding wickedly as she took the second water gun.

The small bell chimed above the entrance again as they stepped back out into the parking lot.

Riley kept a wary watch over her shoulder as they hit the

avenue.

Despite being filled with new hope for the struggle ahead, she was unable to ignore the feeling of dread creeping back into her thoughts.

Because she knew that at any time, the Lawsons could drop them both at a distance.

CHAPTER 33

"Maybe we should set up at one of the neighbors' houses," Taylor huffed as they jogged around the last corner, her cousin's home in sight.

"Yeah, let's get these loaded up first though," Riley shook her empty water gun – the rattling piece of plastic more useless than a pistol without bullets. "Then we'll scope out all the ways they might be coming from."

She scanned the surrounding properties as they walked up the garden path, pondering how she and Keith might have carried out a raid on whoever was holed up inside.

The homes in the housing estate had been built closely together, so there were plenty of windows and fences for their attackers to hide behind. All of the overgrown grass in the area certainly didn't make defending the house any easier either.

"What if they've already been through here?" Taylor hesitated halfway up the concrete porch's steps, glancing sidelong at Riley. "What if they've already set up traps for us inside before they ran off to deal with the fire?" she swallowed, nodding at the door handle, "If they've got a grenade ready to blow on the other side, then we'll be dead the second we try to open this door."

Riley rubbed the back of her neck, considering the possibility for a moment.

A lot of time had passed since they'd heard Demi's final scream in the forest.

Immediately after the interrogation, Stan could have made a beeline for Josh's house and rigged a bunch of deadly surprises inside – long before he even saw the plume of black smoke staining the sky across town.

"You're right," Riley agreed, flexing the slender muscles of her jaw. She had already seen Zack die the moment that he had stepped through a doorway. She wasn't going to let somebody else make that same mistake. Her morning had been eventful enough. They could always come up with another plan. "Let's get the fuck outta here."

She turned to walk back down the garden path, when something zipped past her ear.

In the same instant, an explosion of wooden splinters erupted from the front door.

GUVV!!

A rifle's report smacked their eardrums.

Riley's heart rate revved into overdrive.

She whipped her head around, pupils dilating at the unmistakable sight of Stan Lawson, his ruddy facial bandage in clear view as he lay flat on his stomach at the end of the street.

Cocking another round into the chamber of his sniper rifle, he squinted down the scope again.

"GET DOWN!!" Riley shouted, tackling Taylor to the ground.

Another lead hornet ripped through the air, shattering the master bedroom's window behind them.

Riley hugged the garden path, dust motes swirling with every ragged breath as she hid behind a wall of overgrown grass.

"Stay low," she could barely hear her own voice over the sound of her pulse thundering in her ears. "We can use the grass to crawl around back."

But Taylor was already up and moving.

Abandoning cover, the girl bolted back towards the house, where the fragmented front door had already swung open on its own accord.

Another rifle round followed her inside, punching a hole through the drywall.

Taylor-level dumb, Riley figured bitterly as she spun herself around, still glued to the ground.

She was about to worm her way through the grass, when another gunshot rang out, and she could smell the stench of smoldering fabric wafting behind her.

He can see my backpack, her eyes grew wide with horror.

An empty cartridge *pinged* somewhere down the street as Stan ejected the spent casing.

Without thinking, Riley seized the opportunity.

Adrenaline surging through her veins, she leapt to her feet, sprinting up the path and clearing the porch's steps in a single bound as she plunged inside the house.

She threw herself to the floor of the hall, just as another finger of hot lead tore through the doorway in her wake, showering her in dusty fragments from the drywall.

"I dropped my gun," Taylor blurted out in a panic, crouched beside the wall as she stared outside.

"Forget it – it's gone," Riley grunted as she kicked the ruined door shut behind her, only for it to bounce off the frame before creaking back open again.

"What should we do?" the freckled girl with braces breathed

hard, the fear in her eyes restoring all of the youth that the apocalypse had robbed from her. "We're not ready. I'm not ready. Can't we just run away?"

"There's nowhere to run," Riley gave her the grim truth. She narrowed her eyes down the hall towards the kitchen, "If Stan's out front – that means Everett's out back. They're either gonna flush us out, or they'll come through guns blazing."

Before she could even begin to formulate a plan, something sailed in through the front door, bouncing off the wall.

"OH, FUCK!!" Taylor yelled as a live grenade landed at their feet.

CHAPTER 34

Hearts leaping up into their throats, Riley and Taylor shot to their feet, crashing into each other in their haste to escape the grenade's blast radius.

Awkwardly recovering from the collision, Taylor ducked inside the master bedroom.

Knocked off balance, Riley lurched into the wall before dashing down the hall, diving for cover behind the kitchen's pantry.

BADOOM!!

The entire house shook with the explosion.

Windows shattered from the blast force, while scorching shrapnel flew in every direction, and a thick cloud of black smoke billowed out from the hallway, blanketing the kitchen in a dense haze.

Ears ringing in the aftermath, Riley tried to stagger upright before stumbling sideways, careening back onto the floor again as her rattled brain attempted to recover from the hard reset.

Taylor screamed from somewhere far away, her voice warped and distorted with all the sound sucked out of the air.

As the smoke began to clear, Riley found herself curled up behind the breakfast bar, still clutching the plastic water gun, utterly outclassed by the Lawsons' superior firepower.

She looked around to see small pieces of jagged metal embedded into the surrounding kitchen cabinets, the charred fragments still smoking.

The grenade's explosion had torn gaping holes through the drywall behind her, offering a partial view to the street outside, obscured only by the smoldering wreckage where the hall had once stood.

"FUUUUUCK!!" Taylor's wail of agony pierced through the fading whistling noise. "I can't feel my legs! I can't feel my legs! I can't feel my –"

"Hey, Riley!" Stan's haughty voice cut across the anguished cries of despair. "Are your ears working yet, bitch?"

"Shit, shit, shit," she could barely hear her own voice.

With Taylor crippled in the next room, the girl armed with nothing but a steak knife, Riley was practically on her own against both Everett and Stan.

With a sinking feeling, she knew that she wouldn't be able to make it to the heavy duty chemicals in the laundry.

Not without being seen.

Her eyes darted around the hazy kitchen instead, frantically searching for the sink.

Zeroing in on the metal faucet looming above the countertop, she slid sideways, pulling open the cabinet underneath.

Keenly aware of the shredded drywall exposing her position, she swiped an armful of cleaning chemicals out from the bottom shelf, before retreating back to the corner behind the breakfast bar.

"Demi told me some *nasty* things about you before she died," Stan called, taunting Riley from the curb. "How you left her to fend for herself – she had no chance of escaping with her foot all mangled up like that. She even said that you told her to finish me off while I was face down and unconscious – I guess she just didn't have the heart for it. And, oh yeah, she also told me that YOU KILLED MY FUCKING MOM!!"

Riley ignored him as she scanned the labels of each bottle.

Hand sanitizer refill. Too thick.

Dishwashing liquid. Too weak.

Hospital-grade disinfectant. Lemon scented. Oh yeah. That's gonna sting.

Riley unscrewed the lids of the disinfectant and her water gun, feverishly sloshing the bottle's contents into her plastic weapon's reservoir.

"Taylor, I know you're innocent in all this," Stan's boots scraped up the garden path with a menacing saunter. "I'll tell you what – I'll make you a deal. If you agree to leave peacefully, I'll let you go. I'm just here to give Riley what she deserves. But I'm only gonna give you ten seconds to get your ass out here. What's it gonna be, Taylor?"

"Eat shit and die, motherfucker!" she yelled from the master bedroom, refusing to play into an obvious trap – as if she could even comply fast enough with her legs paralyzed.

"Have it your way then," Stan chuckled to himself as he climbed up the porch's steps. "That works out better for me, actually. See, I don't know if you ungrateful bitches noticed, but I'm in need of a new nose right now. I've already got Demi's, but having three to choose from is a hell of a lot better than just two. Maybe after I take both of yours, the two of you can help me decide which one looks better on me."

Riley's stomach churned at the thought of watching him try on their severed noses, and she forced herself to swallow the bile bubbling in her throat.

Having filled her weapon's reservoir to the brim with cleaning chemicals, she screwed the lid back on, swift but silent, giving the water gun a few pumps to pressurize the chamber.

"I'm sorry – I didn't mean it!" Taylor blurted out, her voice cracking with a sudden change of heart. "I wanna leave peacefully. It's just... I can't walk..."

Mewling sobs rose up from the master bedroom as the crippled girl came to grips with her new reality.

"No, I think you've made your choice pretty clear," Stan's boots crunched over the debris as he entered the hallway, toting his sniper rifle with a sinister smile. Breathing heavily through his mouth, he added, "The only thing you can hope for now is that my dad gets here fast enough to put you both out of your misery. That might not happen for a while though. He's got his hands full cleaning up the mess you left for us."

Everett's still putting out the fire, Riley realized, glancing at the back door with an inaudible sigh of relief. *Thanks for letting us know you're alone, you stupid son of a bitch.*

Brushing stray strands of hair over her ear, she poked her head out from behind the breakfast bar, peering through the shredded dry wall at Stan as he paused beside the master bedroom's doorway.

Supposing that since Taylor wasn't going anywhere, he decided to leave her for later, and he advanced through the house instead, holding his sniper rifle at the ready.

Breathing shallow, Riley brought up the barrel of her water gun, and – without having any sights to go by – she lined up her shot as best as she could.

"Where are you hiding, Riley?" Stan wondered aloud as he turned the corner.

Aiming directly at what was left of his face, she answered him with two rapid fire jets of hospital-grade disinfectant.

But at the last second, he turned his chin, with one spurt hitting his cheek, while the other coated a curtain of his hair as he let off a hasty retaliation.

GUVV!!

Riley jerked backwards as the rifle round ripped a hole clean through the breakfast bar, hot lead catching the end of her weapon's nozzle, warping the barrel into a melted mess of cheap plastic.

Disinfectant began to ooze out from the broken barrel.

And without being able to crank the hand pump, there was no way to pressurize the chamber again.

Fuck, Riley glanced down at the empty bottle of disinfectant in dismay.

Dropping the gun, she reached for the combat knife strapped to her thigh.

But before she could even grip the hilt, Stan sidestepped around the breakfast bar, the barrel of his sniper rifle pointed squarely at her chest.

"Are you serious?" he scoffed at the sight of the broken plastic toy lying on the floor. He shook with stifled panting in place of a laugh. "After everything you've done, after all the shit you've put us through, you thought a *water gun* was gonna save you? I think my dad overestimated you. I'm gonna take my time with you..."

Riley held up her hands in feigned submission, silently watching as the spray of chemicals that had hit his cheek seeped into his bandage, slowly spreading through the gauze towards his crusty wound.

"Lay down on the fl–" Stan couldn't even finish his own sentence as he winced in pain.

His face twitched at the sharp sting, and he took a confused step backwards.

"What the..." the barrel of his sniper rifle wavered as he tried to blink away the chemical burn permeating through his bandage. "What the fuck did you shoot me with!?"

"Like you said – it's just a water gun," Riley shrugged, trying to sound as placid as possible, her gaze downcast as she calculated the distance to his weapon.

"DON'T YOU FUCKING LIE TO ME!!" he roared, scrunching one eye shut against the agony, before noticing the bottles lying scattered across the floor. "Oh, you're gonna pay for that, you stupid bitch."

With a venomous snarl, he stomped Riley square in the chest with the bottom of his boot, sending her crashing backwards against the kitchen cabinets.

Riley fell sideways to the floor, wheezing from the kick.

Despite the amount of pain that Stan was in, he still held the upper hand.

She only had one play left now – let him shoot her.

As long as the bullet wasn't fatal, then in the time that it would take for him to cock another round into the chamber, she would have her window of opportunity.

But if he killed her, then at least she would have been spared the prolonged suffering that Demi had endured.

"What are you gonna do – kill me?" Riley dared, staring back up at him in defiance.

"No," he seethed, jerking the barrel of his sniper rifle towards one of her knees. "I'm gonna keep you alive for as long as possible."

Riley screwed her eyes shut, pulse pounding in her ears as she braced for the pain.

GUVV!!

Screaming filled the kitchen.

But it wasn't coming from Riley.

Her eyelids snapped open.

The rifle round had missed her knee by half an inch.

Not wasting any time to question her luck, she whipped out her combat knife and shot to her feet.

But she was forced to falter as she lunged towards her tormentor.

Screaming and yelling, twisting and turning, grunting and hissing, Stan was desperately trying to throw Taylor off his back as the freckled girl – with her perfectly fine legs wrapped around him – stabbed wildly at the base of his neck with an already-broken steak knife.

Like a crazed animal, Stan swung around again, slamming Taylor backwards into the pantry's ruined shelves.

Seeing her opening, Riley surged forward, shanking him in the stomach with the full length of her combat knife.

Stan sucked in a gasp of terror, his wide eyes staring back at her in stunned silence.

Riley savored the fear scrawled across his face for a moment, before delivering a savage elbow strike to where his nose had once been.

Reveling in his high-pitched yowl of agony, she twisted the blade in his stomach, redoubling her grip on the handle before dragging the serrated teeth across his torso, disemboweling the sadistic psycho with a single sideways slash.

"Fucking took you long enough," Taylor landed on her feet as Stan fell to the floor.

"I had him," Riley gave her a small snort. She stooped to open his throat from ear to ear, finishing the job that Demi should have done last night. "You sure had me going though."

"As long as this fucker believed it," Taylor grinned, before crouching to wrestle the sniper rifle from Stan's dying grip as he hugged it to his chest in his convulsing death throes. "Come on... you piece of shit..."

Riley wiped her knife clean and rose to her feet, listening to his gurgles with grim satisfaction, while watching them struggle as she sheathed her blade.

She was leaning down to help, when Stan managed to pull something free from a pocket of his hunting vest.

Her pupils dilated at the sight of the second grenade clutched in his hand.

"MOVE!!" Riley roared, snatching Taylor up by the arm and hauling her to the back door.

CHAPTER 35

Riley's ears were still ringing as the blood-spattered pair of survivors worked their way across town, moving from one grisly landmark to the next.

They hadn't even waited for the smoke to clear before they were up and staggering away from the scene.

Because they knew that somewhere out there, Everett Lawson was still alive, and he would have heard both of those grenades.

One – and I'll come running, the wild-eyed widower's words rattled around Riley's battered brain. *Two – and I'll kill anything that moves.*

"Which way?" Taylor asked as they reached another intersection, her voice louder than usual.

Riley whirled around, using hand gestures to urge her to stay quiet, knowing that the girl was only compensating for the temporary hearing loss.

Taylor nodded tersely before shooting a nervous glance over her shoulder.

Turning back to the intersection again, Riley peered at the supermarket's parking lot on the other side of the avenue, the concrete no-man's-land unchanged with its decomposing corpses and overturned shopping carts.

She tapped Taylor before rounding the corner, both of them flitting from one scorched shell of a police vehicle to the next, not even aware of how much noise they were making.

Riley crouched beside the rear of an overturned cruiser, thumbing the straps of her backpack as she glanced left and right, checking for any signs of movement along the avenue before leading Taylor down a side street.

Following the road's curve through the abandoned neighborhood, Riley couldn't help but think that just yesterday – along with Heather, Zack, Austin and Dylan – she had walked the exact same path, without the fear of being hunted down by a merciless Green Beret voracious for vengeance.

A rash of gooseflesh budded up her arms, and she shot a glance back towards the avenue, fast enough to startle Taylor, the wide-eyed girl taking cover behind the nearest tree trunk.

Not knowing whether they were being watched or not, the constant weight of dread was almost heavy enough to crush them both, with the ringing in their ears only adding to the eerie stillness hanging in the air.

Pressing on along the silent street, they warily approached the mouth of a cul-de-sac, and Riley allowed herself to breathe a small sigh of relief as they gazed at the double-story weatherboard home on the corner.

A new plan was forming in her mind as she peered up at an open set of curtains on the second story, speculating that the upper level's windows would offer a decent vantage point over the rest of the neighborhood.

It wasn't much of a strategy – but if they could manage to keep a low profile down in the well-stocked basement until Heather's leg healed up, then in a few months, they could take a chance on leaving the town, putting as much distance between them and Everett as possible.

They could ration their food, set up water catchments behind the back gate, and silently bide their time until they were ready to move again.

Riley drew a galvanizing breath and nodded to herself in silence, as if she was physically committing to her own plan.

Cautiously glancing over her shoulder again, she led Taylor across the street and up the stone retaining wall's stairs.

Although their hearing hadn't yet fully returned, they were still mindful of their shoes making any noise as they walked up the garden path.

Riley had her sights set on the downward-sloping driveway, intending to go around back, when Taylor broke off, bounding up onto the veranda lined with dead pot plants.

Overcome with longing to see her big sister again, she pushed open the front door and swept into the hallway, beaming around as she poked her head into the living room and the office, before craning her neck to look upstairs.

Riley followed her inside, scanning the street one last time before shutting the door and twisting the deadbolt, frowning slightly at why it hadn't been locked in the first place.

Dylan, she supposed, shaking her head. *Looks like we're gonna have to teach that kid how to protect what he's got.*

"Where is she?" Taylor tapped her on the shoulder, conscious of her own voice this time.

"This way," Riley led her over to the basement door, cracking it open and peering down the wooden staircase. "Heather, are you still in here? Why wasn't the front door locked?"

But there was no reply.

Riley flexed her gloved fingers as the silence stretched.

Then, an ominous thud sounded from below.

She shot Taylor a sidelong glance, both of them feeling the dread creeping back into their thoughts again.

"Took you guys long enough," Heather's husky voice finally floated up to greet them. "Tell me you found my sister, and you're not just coming back here because you ran outta food."

With a squeal of delight, Taylor pushed past Riley and hurried down the stairs, not even momentarily distracted by the wall of shelves lined with supplies as she rushed to hug her sister.

Riley followed her down into the L-shaped basement to see Heather sitting on the old floral-print couch underneath the staircase, her wounded leg elevated on the wooden table beside a hardcover book.

"Fucking hell, Taylor, take it easy," Heather chuckled even as she winced in pain, wrestling her little sister onto the seat beside her.

"I didn't think I'd ever see you again," Taylor buried her face into Heather's shoulder, still refusing to let her go.

"What did I say about you thinking?" Heather teased, wiping away a tear. "You leave that to me." She looked up at Riley with a glad smile, "Thank you so much. I knew you'd bring her back safe."

"For a while there, I wasn't so sure," Riley admitted as she unshouldered her backpack, dropping it in the patch of sunlight offered by the two small windows set in the far wall.

They held each other's gaze for a long moment, and Riley's tightly-wound shoulders slackened as she felt a wave of relief washing over her, the burden of her moral debt to the Seabrook sisters finally paid in full.

But in the back of her mind – even if she hadn't been partly responsible for splitting them up in the first place – she knew that somehow, she would have aligned herself with Heather and the rest of her group regardless.

Because they were good people.

And it was a rarity to find good people these days.

"Where are the others?" Heather broke the silence, one arm around her sister as she stared up at the underside of the wooden staircase, expecting more sets of footsteps to come shuffling down into the basement.

"We ran into some trouble out there," Riley's gaze fell to the wounded woman's leg. "Those guys who set up that trap in the alley – that wasn't the only one." She shook her head solemnly, "Your friends didn't make it."

"Fuck," Heather swallowed, her eyes turning downcast, realizing that she had sent Zack and Austin to their deaths. She hugged Taylor close, smelling her hair and blinking hard before whispering softly in her ear, "As long as you're safe. That's all that matters. You're the only one I care about."

Taylor nodded meekly as she drew back, brushing her cheeks dry as she glanced around the room for the first time.

"Is that real?" she shot to her feet, wiping her eyes again, unable to believe what she was seeing. She looked back at her sister before staring in awe at the bounty of food lining the shelves along the wall. "How the hell did you find all this?"

"I guess you guys just weren't looking hard enough," Heather shared a sidelong smirk with Riley. "We've only been in town for a couple of days."

"Bullshit," Taylor called her out on the lie with half a laugh, glancing down skeptically at her sister's wounded leg before looking over at Riley. "There's no way you two could've gotten all this by yourselves."

"She doesn't believe us," Riley frowned at Heather as she

joined in on the joke. They shared a snort of amusement, before she gave voice to the question that had been on her mind since they had entered the basement, "Hey, where's the kid, anyway?"

"He got up before me," Heather shrugged from the couch, glancing down at the pair of mattresses on the other side of the table. "I heard him upstairs a little while ago. I haven't seen him since though."

"What kid?" Taylor's face darkened, swallowing her smile as she turned to face them both. Her gaze went from Riley to Heather as she backed herself up against the shelves. "What – fucking – kid?"

As if to answer her question, something heavy fell against the basement's back door.

CHAPTER 36

"It's not budging," Riley grunted and strained against the hardwood door, the basement echoing as she rammed her shoulder into the back exit again.

"What fucking kid!?" Taylor shouted incessantly, breathing rapidly as her eyes filled with panic.

"Calm down," Heather huffed with a frown as she drew her black leather office chair closer to the couch. "Just some kid named Dylan. He brought us all down here and –"

"Oh, fuck, fuck, fuck, we are so fucked," Taylor paced the room, running her hands through her hair in dismay. "We have to go. We have to go – right now!"

"Heather's not going anywhere if we can't get that door unblocked," Riley skirted around the pair of mattresses as she crossed the basement. She picked up her backpack, slinging it over one shoulder as she set foot on the wooden staircase. "I'm gonna go around the front and see what's on the other side."

She glanced up at the hallway as her boots drummed up the stairs.

But her pupils dilated, and she froze in terror.

The barrel of an assault rifle was staring back at her.

Instinctively, she ducked down, just as a burst of bullets blasted into the basement.

The three rifle rounds ripped through the air, slamming into a stack of canned food on the shelves behind her, with flash-fried soup oozing out from the shredded metal.

Adrenaline pumping through her veins, Riley threw herself to the floor, falling onto her backpack before scrambling around the corner and taking cover behind the wall.

"He's here!" Taylor cried, wrenching Heather's exposed leg off the table and pulling it back underneath the staircase.

"You didn't check if you were being followed!?" Heather snarled in pain at her sister's rough handling.

Cut off from the other two, Riley breathed shallow with her back against the wall.

To her left was the pair of small windows set just below the ceiling, but even if she had something to stand on to reach them, the narrow frames would have made it impossible for her to squeeze through.

Her heart sank as she realized that there was only one way they were getting out – and that was by rushing headlong up the staircase through a hail of bullets.

"Show me your face again, Riley," Everett rasped, his voice thick and raw with grief. Heavy footfalls marched towards the doorway, and he added, "I dare you."

"No, I'm good right here," she rose to her feet, unslinging her backpack as one hand dropped to the combat knife strapped to her thigh. "Why don't you come down?"

"What kind of sick fucks don't even let a man bury his own family?" Everett seethed as he ignored her invitation, keeping distance to his advantage. "We took you in and gave you girls an opportunity – a chance at getting back to the way things used to be – better than anything you could've hoped for after the world went to shit. And this is how you thank us?"

"You didn't give us a choice!" Taylor yelled from around the corner. "We were doing just fine on our own, and then you and your psycho family turned us into your fucking slaves!"

"Helping out with chores around the house – you thought *that* was slavery?" he rumbled from the hallway. "You haven't seen half the shit I've seen. And that was from *before* everything fell apart."

Riley's ears pricked up as she heard something scraping across the floor.

Still staying behind cover, she leaned out sideways to see Taylor dragging one of the mattresses into the basement's far corner.

"Keep talking," Taylor mouthed silently at her before straining to pick up the mattress, leaning it up against the wall.

"How'd you find us?" Riley bought her some time, playing along with whatever the two sisters were planning. She swallowed as her gaze went up to the ceiling, hoping that presenting an opportunity for him to gloat would be enough to lure him into continuing the conversation. "We would've been long gone by the time you made it over to Josh's house."

"But you did what people always do when they know they can't win," Everett took the bait, "Go to ground, and hope that it all blows over. When my son's second grenade..." he trailed off for a moment, clearing his throat before continuing, "I knew you'd come back here. By the time you came in through the front door, I was already upstairs, waiting for you to head down into the basement."

"Hold on, how'd you know about this place?" Riley furrowed her eyebrows. Her tongue pressed against the inside of her cheek as she realized, "That fucking kid…"

"You think it's a coincidence that this basement happens to be full of food?" Everett asked with a rhetorical jeer. "Those shelves – I stocked them myself. That body upstairs reaching for his meds – that's not where we found him. This is just another one of our traps. Dylan knows the drill. He finds people who might be useful, leads them to a spot where they'll stay the longest, and then he lets us know. Stan saw his signal yesterday."

"What fucking signal?" Taylor broke in, overcome with spiteful curiosity.

Riley chanced another glance around the corner.

The two sisters had leaned the pair of mattresses up against the far wall, intending to hide behind them for cover.

Riley motioned for Taylor to turn the makeshift barricade flat against the other wall, so that they would have more cushion standing in between them and the staircase.

"The curtains are the signal, one window per –" Everett stopped mid-sentence as he heard the pair of mattresses scratching across the floor.

Riley's breathing hitched.

He knew that they were up to something.

With her back against the wall, she shut her eyes as she heard the wheels of Heather's office chair rolling into the basement's far corner, the sound almost deafening.

The staircase creaked as Everett slowly ventured down to investigate.

Riley could feel death approaching with his every step in the dread-filled silence.

CHAPTER 37

"Clever," Everett Lawson admitted from the top of the staircase, wise to their efforts to distract him now. "That might be enough to stop bullets from a pistol. But my rifle's gonna rip that to shreds. Watch."

Riley drew a galvanizing breath as his weapon rattled towards the Seabrook sisters.

Cold adrenaline rushing through her veins, she lunged towards the shelves, grabbed a stack of cans and launched them up the stairs, the volley striking him in the side.

The bloodthirsty Green Beret growled, and he turned his assault rifle on her instead.

Pupils dilating, Riley dove for cover behind the wall again, with a burst of hot lead rocketing into the shelves in her wake.

"I'm the one you want!" she shouted as she scrambled to her feet, bargaining for Heather and Taylor's lives before he could take aim at them again. "I killed your wife. I started the fire that burned down your house. Stan blew himself up after I slit his throat. My friends haven't done shit to you and your family!"

"Yeah – you are the one I want," Everett agreed, holding his position at the top of the staircase. "I want you to feel what it's like to lose the only people you have left. I want you to look at their dead bodies, knowing that in spite of everything you did to protect them, it still wasn't enough. After you admit that you failed them – that's when I'll kill you."

Riley flexed the slender muscles of her jaw.

She only had one option left.

Whipping out her combat knife, she coiled herself into a sprinter's pose beside the corner, summoning the insanity to rush headlong up the stairs.

Everett's weapon rattled again as he swept the barrel towards the pair of mattresses.

Clenching the combat knife in her gloved fist, she was about to lunge forward, when in the corner of her eye, Taylor dashed out from behind cover, screaming towards Riley.

The basement thundered with automatic gunfire as a barrage of bullets tore after her, the stream of death punching lead slugs into the shelves, with sacks of flour and rice bleeding out onto the floor.

Eyes wide with fear, Taylor ran straight into Riley, knocking her off balance and sending them both sprawling to the ground.

"What the fuck, Taylor!?" Riley shoved her to one side, drawing herself up into a crouch again.

"Give me a boost," she urged, breathlessly glancing at the pair of windows below the ceiling. "I'll fit through and then we can outflank him. Come on!"

Another roar of rifle rounds sucked all the sound out of the basement.

Riley's heart froze as she stared across the length of the room.

Fragments of foam and fibers floated in the far corner as the pair of mattresses sagged, riddled with bullet holes.

The back of Heather Seabrook's office chair trundled out halfway, wedged in between the wall and the ruined barricade.

A breath of disbelief escaped Riley's lips as her vision swam with the somber sight.

All Heather had wanted to do was reunite with her little sister.

She had never even met the Lawson Family.

Heather was innocent.

She didn't deserve to die.

"YOU MOTHERFUCKER!!" Riley exploded out from behind the wall, surging up the stairs as Everett dropped his spent magazine.

But the merciless brute had anticipated the attack.

Reacting with lightning speed reflexes, Everett jumped over the staircase's handrail, discarding his empty assault rifle and drawing his pistol before his boots even hit the floor.

"There it is," he held his handgun trained on Riley, savoring the outrage in her eyes. His face was still painted in mottled shades of forest green, only now it was blackened by the smoke of his burnt home. "Toss the blade and stand next to Taylor. *Slowly.*"

"Fuck that," she snarled, burning her stare into the wild-eyed widower's gaze.

"Or I could just blow out your kneecaps," Everett shrugged, although he kept his aim trained squarely at her chest. "You can slump down next to Taylor instead. Makes no difference to me."

Shaking with adrenaline, Riley's thoughts raced for an alternative.

Another plan.

A weakness that she could exploit.

But her mind kept drawing blanks.

178

The unwavering Green Beret was too smart.

Too quick.

Too strong.

One step out of line, and she was dead on her feet.

But if she couldn't think of something soon, she was dead anyway.

"What's it gonna be, Riley?" Everett prompted her, ruthless and relentless. "I'll tell you what – if you make this quick for me, I'll make it quick for you. But that's not what you deserve, so I'm hoping you take the other option. The one where you still think you're the hero in all this. You try to fight. You try to run. You try to hide. And I will fill the rest of your miserable little life with the most excruciating pain imaginable. You'll be begging for death before we even get through the first month."

"Riley, could you..." Taylor's voice quavered, trembling with anguish over the loss of her sister, coupled with knowing that she was the next in line to die. "Could you hold my hand?"

The girl's eyes were brimming with tears.

She was trying so hard to stay strong.

All the fight left Riley then.

The combat knife slipped from her hand, clattering onto the staircase.

With leaden feet, she climbed down the steps, peeling off her gloves and dropping them to the floor in resignation.

Riley felt the cold eye of the pistol's barrel following her every move as she took Taylor's hand with her scarred fingers, trying to set the whimpering girl at ease before their deaths.

"Anything you wanna say?" Everett asked as he held Taylor at gunpoint.

"Yeah, just one thing," she swallowed a sob before glancing sidelong at Riley, her mask of sorrow twisting into a spiteful scowl. "Dylan's next."

Before Riley could even process the statement, a sudden tug on her hand pulled her to the floor as Taylor dropped to her knees, and a hardcover book sailed across the room, catching Everett full in the face.

CRACK!

His bullet veered off course, and the brawny Green Beret stood momentarily dumbfounded, searching for the third hostile in the room.

Taylor seized advantage of his distraction, charging across the basement and tackling his trigger arm, another stray round shattering a jar of preserves as she tried to wrestle the weapon out of his grip.

Everett rasped and growled in annoyance, grappling with her for a moment before reaching for his combat knife with his other hand.

An icy shot of adrenaline bolted through Riley's veins, and she rushed headlong towards his other arm, slamming his blade back into its sheath before twisting his hand behind his back.

"You're not the only one who can set up a trap, bitch," Heather Seabrook's snarl sliced through the sounds of struggle as she climbed out from behind the couch underneath the staircase. She hopped over to his discarded assault rifle, "Riley, get me some ammo!"

Stunned by the fiery redhead's sudden reappearance, Riley snapped herself out of her stupor, and with one hand holding Everett's arm pinned behind his back, she fumbled with the front of his tactical vest, ripping out a fresh magazine and tossing it at Heather's feet.

The wild-eyed widower watched as Heather stooped to reload his weapon, and he emptied his pistol's remaining bullets at the ground, freeing up his hand to throw Taylor off, smashing the side of her skull into the shelves, the girl slumping to the floor.

Riley tangled her boots around his ankle, leaning all of her weight as she pulled him off balance, but not before he could kick the assault rifle out of Heather's grip, sending it skittering across the floor to the other side of the basement.

Everett fell on top of Riley, and he twisted his arm out of her grip.

Pulling his combat knife free, he lunged for her throat with a downward stab.

Relying on pure instinct, Riley slammed her forearm up into his, blocking the blow.

But pinned to the floor underneath the big brawny bear of a man, the tip of his blade steadily inched closer, yearning to spear through her windpipe.

The full extent of the bloodthirsty brute's savagery was scrawled plainly across his camouflage-painted face, his eyes wide and foaming at the mouth as he snarled and roared and drove his knife towards her throat.

Riley's other arm was trapped in between her chest and his tactical vest, with the rigid metal of his spare magazines dragging along the back of her hand.

She had almost slipped her knuckles free of a fist-sized bulge, when she recognized the shape of a metal ring.

A grenade, she realized, almost dropping her defense completely as she considered expending the last ounces of her strength to pull the pin.

It would mean certain death for her, the contained blast butchering both of their bodies, but at least Heather and Taylor would survive.

Riley winced as the tip of Everett's combat knife licked at her throat, and with a primal roar, she pushed back with everything she had, freeing her other hand to fumble for his grenade's pull ring.

But before she could thread her finger through, Everett grunted in pain, and he eased off the attack, setting his sights on a new target instead.

Heather was looming over them both, the fiery redhead drawing her arm up to crown the back of his skull with another pistol whip.

He slashed at her legs, forcing her to jump backwards.

Heather landed on both feet, a bolt of agony surging up her injured leg, and she fell sideways with a guttural scream.

With both hands now free, Riley grabbed hold of Everett's outstretched blade arm, twisting his wrist around until he was forced to roll onto his back.

Leaping up onto his chest, she sunk one knee into his other shoulder as she rammed his knife hand against the floor.

But he had an iron grip around the hilt of his blade.

In an act of sheer desperation, Riley brought his fist up to her face, and she sank her teeth into the base of his little finger.

Clamping her jaws tight, she *squeezed*, a hot gush of blood flooding into her mouth.

She gnawed through the flesh of his finger all the way to the bone.

Bellowing in agony, his grip faltered, and the weapon fell to the floor.

Snatching up the combat knife, she turned his own blade against him, snarling like a feral beast as she thrust the tip towards the base of his neck.

Everett caught her wrist with his bleeding hand, his weakened grip still holding firm as he fought her for control over the knife.

"Hold still for a second," Riley growled in exertion, fire in her eyes. "You're about to see the rest of your fucked up family again."

A shadow fell across his painted-green face, and his pupils dilated at the sight of something over her shoulder.

"Don't waste your time," Heather chided, wrapping her hands around Riley's grip from behind and adding all of her bodyweight on top of the downward thrust. Their combined strength overpowered him, and they sunk the blade deep into the side of his windpipe. "Go for the throat. *And then cross him the fuck –*"

But before she could finish her sentence, Everett let out a primordial roar, even as his blood sprayed their faces. Drawing up one of his legs, he kicked the heel of his boot into Riley's rear, lifting up the pair of women with an unprecedented burst of strength.

Suspending them both in midair, he pried their fingers off the knife before throwing their bodies up and over his head, sending them both sprawling across the floor.

Riley craned her neck, her legs tangled up with Heather's, watching in disbelief as the hulking Green Beret reared up again, towering above them with his maimed hand holding the knife in place, staunching the blood pulsing from his throat.

Glowering down at them both – the relentless revenant ravenous for revenge – his other hand reached for the pull pin of his grenade.

"Hey, motherfucker!!" Taylor's shout filled the basement as she cradled his assault rifle, blood trickling down the side of her face. "Anything you wanna say!?"

She didn't wait for an answer.

CHAPTER 38

"Come on, it can't be that bad," Taylor huffed as she helped her hobbling sister over to the old floral-print couch underneath the stairs.

"You think so?" Heather bristled as she sat down with a grimace, her leg's bandage bloody from the fight. "I can show you where we found that alley. Let's see how far you can walk after you get hit by a row of spikes."

"Where's the antiseptic that Zack was using yesterday?" Riley asked as she rummaged through their medical supplies, setting aside fresh bandages to treat their wounds.

They had draped a bed sheet over Everett's bullet-riddled corpse, but his tactical vest and all of his weapons had been laid out across the wooden table.

"If you can't find it, do you wanna try that home remedy instead?" Heather wondered, glancing pointedly at a jar of honey sitting on one of the shelves.

"I wouldn't risk it on your leg," Riley knew that Heather just wanted to pay her respects to her fallen friends, but they couldn't chance an infection – especially if the healing properties of honey turned out to be a medical myth. "For that cut on Taylor's head though..."

They shared a snicker across the room.

"Sure, laugh at the girl who just saved your asses," Taylor narrowed her eyes for a moment, although she couldn't help but chuckle herself.

"Hey, did I hear you right earlier?" Heather raised her eyebrows at Riley. "Are we really calling each other friends now?"

"People say stupid shit when they're about to die," Riley kept her reply guarded as she pulled out a handful of medicine bottles, studying each label in the light.

"Oh, you mean like when we were out on the road?" Heather snorted with a twitch of her eyebrows. "Not a single day went by that I didn't think we were about to die – ever since you and me left Colorado in the middle of winter. Now, I'm just numb to it."

"Come to think about it, I've felt the same way," Riley smiled back at her, hearing the unspoken message.

They shared a nod, just as a wooden clatter sounded from outside.

Slowly, the basement's back door creaked open.

Riley and Taylor were on their feet in a flash.

"Is it over, you guys?" Dylan poked his head through the doorway, staring around the room and flinching at the sight of Everett's corpse.

"It's about to be," Taylor snatched up the assault rifle, taking aim at Dylan.

"Wait, wait, wait!" the curly-haired kid held up his hands in surrender. "Mr Lawson made me do it – all of it. And Stan too. They said they'd kill me if I didn't!"

"Bullshit," Taylor stared along the top of the rifle's barrel at him. "I don't believe a word that comes outta your mouth. You fucking tricked me and Demi into following you up into that treehouse. And now all of our friends are dead. Give me one good reason why I shouldn't just waste you right now."

Heather hugged her injured leg to her chest, watching with indifference, having seen her little sister kill complete strangers for less.

But Riley knocked the rifle's barrel aside, a burst of bullets punching into the wall instead.

"What the fuck!?" Taylor scowled sidelong at her, "He deserves to die for what he did."

"He knew exactly what you guys were walking into yesterday," Heather nodded in agreement. "He's probably the worst of them. He helped me with my leg. Made me lunch. Found me a book to read. And then he gave them a signal to come get me. He's gotta go."

"I know, but he's just a kid," Riley let out a pained sigh as she reluctantly spoke in his favor. She turned to Taylor, "You don't want his death weighing on your conscience – regardless of what he's done. It'll eat away at you for the rest of your life. Trust me. I've seen it happen."

Riley paused, swallowing as she remembered Keith Bowman's burden – the ghost of a five-year-old boy from the worst night of his career – still following the former policeman wherever he went.

"Besides," she continued, "They could've told him anything. Who's to say he wasn't just mind-fucked into leading a bunch of people to their deaths?"

She locked eyes with Heather, reminding her of how they had both been manipulated, slaughtering dozens of innocents in exchange for a buffet breakfast at the Leadthorne Riverfront

Hotel.

"Fine," Taylor heaved a begrudging sigh, finally agreeing to lower the weapon.

"T–t–thanks, you guys," Dylan stammered as he lowered his arms to his sides again, still fearfully gazing at Taylor. "So, does that mean I can stay here? I'd probably die out there if I have to look for food all by myself."

"Not our problem, you lying little snake," Heather scoffed at the idea of sheltering somebody who had sold them out. "I'll bet you've got another stash hidden somewhere around town. Grab that on your way out. You can dupe the next group of suckers into feeding you."

"If I ever see you again, I'll nail you in the fucking face," Taylor promised as she jerked the assault rifle up at him again. "You're lucky you're just a kid. Feel free to come back when you're older though."

"P–p–please, Riley?" Dylan lingered in the doorway despite being held at gunpoint, begging for them to reconsider.

"That story about your sister – was any of that true?" Riley cocked an eyebrow at him. "Did Nancy ever even exist?"

Dylan stared down at the ground, as if the answer was written around his shoes.

"Nancy was the name of my dog," he finally admitted, unable to look at any of them in the eye. "She died a long time ago."

"Get lost, kid," Riley narrowed her eyes in disgust, tossing him a can of soup to send him on his way.

She watched from the back steps as he trudged up the driveway and out onto the street, making sure that he was really leaving.

"We can't stay here," Taylor gave voice to what they were all thinking. Dylan knowing their location was a liability. She gazed up at the shelves lining the wall, "It's gonna take us forever to move all this."

Riley took a deep breath, knowing that they would also have to find another suitable place to spend the next few months while Heather's leg healed up.

She glanced down at the weather-beaten shopping cart parked beside the back steps – probably the vehicle that the Lawson Family had used to transport their victims back to their property along the highway.

"Heather, do you think you could start a fire?" she called over her shoulder as she wrestled the shopping cart back into the basement.

"I can, but... why?" Heather tilted her head with curiosity.

"Because if we're moving all this shit after what we just did," Riley glanced pointedly at all of their supplies, "Then I'm gonna need a bucket-sized cup of coffee first."

* * *

Keep reading to receive an email when the next book gets published!

Find out what happens next!

Thank you so much for reading Predators of The Fall. I hope you enjoyed the story.

Join my newsletter here to receive an email when the next book gets published!
www.steveheuzinkveld.com/newsletter

I'd also like to invite you to my Book Lovers Facebook Group. Chat with me, have a character named after you, talk with other fans, and win exclusive prizes and giveaways.
Join the fun!
www.facebook.com/groups/SteveHeuzinkveldVIPFans

Here's a QR code so you don't have to type out any links:

ACKNOWLEDGMENTS

As always, first and foremost, I want to thank my beautiful wife, Hariezoy, for supporting me and encouraging me every single day, and for giving me the freedom to burn the midnight oil to hit the keyboard every night until the sun comes up.

A huge thanks also goes to my Patreon followers, Greg Hyndman, Rupert Lugo and Martin Georgiev. Your continued support has really helped soften the financial impact in hiring professional artists for my book covers, the ongoing website costs, and all of the other expenses that it takes to keep this author's dreams alive!

I'd like to thank all of the preppers and home defense enthusiasts who made great suggestions for barricades and traps to include in the story – in particular, Randy Norris, Brandon Jakubowski, Gage Laykin, Tom Brooks, Todd Sprague, Stephen Sosack, Randy Mouser, Kelci Ann, Wayne Mikel and Rowan Riffraff. No raiders will ever reach your stockpiles!

I also want to give a massive shout-out to Devlin Odd, Johanna Murphy, Kody Schvaneveldt, Verchie Totanes, Peter Kelly, Mary Drotar, Crystal Capponi, Joanne LeBlanc, Corinne Marshall, Reattha Chapman and Cindy Schmid. Every week, I'll look at the reactions to my books, and seeing your names with absolutely stellar feedback always makes my day. I'm truly blessed to have such awesome readers!

And last but not least, thank you. As an independently-published author, this is very often a one-man show, and after the hours upon hours I've invested into this project, it means the world to me that you've taken the time to meet the characters living in my head.

I'd love to put your name here in my future books, right alongside Greg, Rupert and Martin. Join us on Patreon for access to never-before-seen chapters from my other works, as well as autographed copies of future books, all while helping me to bring more stories to life!

www.patreon.com/SteveHeuzinkveld

Be sure to follow me on Amazon to receive a notification when my next book releases!

www.amazon.com/Steve-Heuzinkveld/e/B09FZFK2XW

P.S. I love hearing from my fans - feel free to contact me any time!

-Steve
author@SteveHeuzinkveld.com
www.SteveHeuzinkveld.com